SLAIN AT THE SEA

A MADDIE MILLS COZY MYSTERY

CINDY BELL

CHAPTER 1

"*O*kay, girls! Time to check out your new home!"

Maddie Mills scooped up the small dogs, one by one, out of the backseat of her SUV and helped them down onto the ground. The West Highland White Terriers sniffed at the dirt driveway, then looked up at Maddie with wide eyes.

"I know, I know, it smells weird. Everything is going to be a little different. But as long as we're together, it's going to be just fine. Come on, Bella and Polly."

Maddie grabbed their leashes and headed toward the porch. A loud creak echoed through Maddie's ears as she stepped on the floorboard of the dusty, front steps.

"Welcome home, Maddie." She looked over the

large, filthy windows that framed the ancient, green door. She recalled the last time her mother had painted it. As a young girl, she'd thought the color was so bright that it would never fade. Although it had faded a bit, it was still bright.

The home had been in her family for a long time, and after her mother's death years ago, she hadn't been able to return to it. As a mother juggling three kids and a husband, she had been overwhelmed by the loss of her mother and couldn't handle the thought of walking through the door of the house without hearing her mother call out a greeting.

Now, at forty-eight, Maddie was back at the house she had grown up in, a house she hadn't returned to in years. It wasn't the only thing that had gathered dust while she wasn't paying attention. She'd once believed that her life was as glossy and bright as that fresh coat of green paint on the front door had been. But during her divorce a few months before and her ex-husband's subsequent arrest, she discovered that things were not as squeaky clean as she had once imagined.

"I guess I have quite a bit of cleaning to do, now." Maddie swept her gaze up to the second story. "Nothing that a bit of cleaning won't fix."

Maddie led the dogs up to the front door. She slid a key into the lock and held her breath as she wondered if it would even turn. A second later, the lock gave way, and the door swung open. She braced herself, still half-expecting to hear her mother's sing-song voice call out. She was always thrilled when they visited.

"Move back here, Maddie, Bayview is a great place to raise kids, and you and I will get to spend so much time together."

Back then, in her twenties, with two toddlers and an infant, the idea of moving back to the tiny town of Bayview sounded like a prison sentence, not a paradise. Now, after more than twenty more years of life, she understood her mother's desire. She wished her own children lived close to her, and now that her first grandchild was born, she loved the idea of getting to see her every day. But life hadn't panned out that way. In the end, her mother had come to live with her in her last years of life. It wasn't what she had planned, but she had enjoyed her final years with Maddie and her grandchildren.

Maddie hoped that getting the big house cleaned up and making it her home, might turn it into a place where her family could join together for the holidays and reunions, but it was far from that at the moment. She looked around at the furniture covered in once-white sheets.

Amber West had done all of that for her. Her best childhood friend, they had drifted apart when they went off to college, but when Maddie's mother had died, she was right there to get done what needed to be done. Again, they had drifted apart. She smiled as she looked forward to seeing her again.

Maddie held the leashes of the eager dogs and mounted the stairs that led to the second floor.

She smiled as she passed a collection of photographs on the wall. Her parents, her as a child, her younger sister, their lives together. She ran her fingertips through the layer of dust on the surface of the glass and uncovered her bright, eight-year-old grin. How different things had looked, then. How different things looked, now. She continued down the hall across the floorboards.

Maddie paused outside the door that had been her childhood bedroom. Lacey curtains still covered the window that overlooked the bay below. She'd spent hours curled up in that window, reading, and looking out over the water as she imagined how her life would unfold. Many things had been better than she could imagine, like her wonderful children, and the adventures she shared with her husband. But things between her and her husband had certainly taken a darker turn than she ever anticipated.

"Craig, why did you have to keep so many secrets?" Maddie pulled back the curtain and looked out through the window.

She looked out over the bay. She never thought she'd be back here, back in the place where she'd started. She glanced down at the dogs. At least she had Bella and Polly with her.

Maddie recalled how loud the house had been when she was a little girl. Her parents loved music and would dance through the living room. They always encouraged her and her sister, Tammy, to be lively and sing loud. She had passed on the same vibrancy to her own children.

"Okay, time to get some noise in here." She unhooked the dogs' leashes, satisfied that the house was safe to inhabit, and walked down the stairs with them close behind.

Then something caught the dogs' attention, and they both bolted for the kitchen.

"Bella, Polly!" Maddie gasped as she hurried after them. "What are you chasing, you curious pups?"

It didn't take her long to discover exactly what, as a face appeared in the frosted glass of the back door. Her heart jumped with surprise at the sight. As far as she knew, no one was aware that she had returned to Bayview, other than Amber.

"Hello?" Maddie froze as she tried to see through the distorted glass.

A light knock sounded on the back door. "Maddie? Is that you?"

Instantly she relaxed. If he knew her name, then there was a good chance he had a legitimate reason for being there. She unlocked the door and opened it. She immediately recognized the man on the other side of the screen door.

"Mr. Wilson!" She laughed as she gazed at the

older man. He had to be in his seventies and although he had aged, he still looked much younger than seventy. "I didn't expect to see you here."

"Oh, I've been keeping an eye on the place for you. Keeping the critters out and making sure the roof stays up." Barry Wilson grinned. "Amber told me you'd be coming home today, so I thought I'd stop by." He gestured to the path behind the house that led down to the bay. "I always come this way, it's easier from my house than coming by the road. Sorry, if I startled you."

"Not at all, come inside if you'd like. I'm afraid I don't have much in the way of groceries, yet. I just had the power turned on this morning, so it's going to take some time before I'm ready for guests." Maddie stepped back to allow him room to step inside. The dogs took up the room immediately, eager to make a new friend.

"Oh, I'm not a guest, you know that. We've been neighbors for decades. And who are these beautiful pups?" Barry crouched down and held his hands out to them.

"Bella and Polly." Maddie smiled as the dogs lapped at his hands. "They are moving in, too."

"Good to meet you, girls." Barry gave them each a pat on the head. As he stood up, he met Maddie's eyes. "It's good to see you home again, Maddie. I know your mother would be thrilled."

Maddie smiled. She wished she could say she was thrilled. She was trying, but moving back home felt less like a choice, and more like her only option.

CHAPTER 2

"Can I help you bring anything in from the car?" Barry started toward the front door.

"Actually, there's not much to get." Maddie followed him into the living room. "There's lots of furniture already here, so I just brought the necessities."

"I always thought you'd sell this place." Barry pulled back one of the white sheets from an old, wooden chair. "I guess after they built the highway, you couldn't get much for it."

"No, not a dime." Maddie pulled a sheet off the claw-foot couch she had spent much of her childhood sprawled across. "But things seem to be improving around here. I noticed the updates to the marina, and that there are a few new businesses in town."

"It's all because of the incentives and grants." Barry turned to face her. "We've been working hard to get Bayview back on the map. So many people lost so much when the highway was built. So many businesses suffered and closed due to the decrease in traffic coming through town, and of course property values tanked. But now they've built a new scenic route that runs right through town, we're hoping that will drive some more business our way. The expansion of the marina means that larger, luxury boats can dock there. I think it's all going to keep improving."

"Wow, that's a lot of changes." Maddie sat down on one side of the couch. Instantly, Bella and Polly jumped up beside her. One on either side. "I'm so glad that things have begun to turn around."

"It's all thanks to a few people working very hard to get the attention of the local government and get these grants approved. I didn't think I'd live to see the day when people started moving to Bayview again, but here I am." Barry grinned as he sat down on the other side of the couch. He could barely fit with the two dogs spread out on it. "Of course, not everyone is happy about it."

"I'm sure." Maddie gave a short laugh as she imagined some of the reactions from the locals. "Not everyone is going to want tourists wandering around here."

"So stuck in their ways." Barry clucked his tongue. "I say, anything that gets businesses back open, is a good thing. Speaking of businesses, the bakery your parents owned is still standing. Although, abandoned.

Do you own that now? I wasn't sure if it had changed hands."

"Along with my sister." Maddie pet the two dogs that climbed all over the couch, trying to get closer to her. "Alright, settle down now, girls, I know this is all very exciting."

"Are you going to open it up again?" Barry's eyes shined as he looked at her.

"I hadn't really thought about it." Maddie frowned. "Honestly, I haven't thought too much further than getting back here. I have to get the house cleaned up, I'm not sure if I could take on another project. And I'm certainly not as good a baker as my mother was."

"Well, if you could, now would be the time." Barry stood up from the couch and gave each of the dogs another pat. "Businesses are starting to take off, and I'm sure everyone around here would love to see the Bayview Bakery reopened. Let me know if there's anything I can do to help. Remember, I'm just down the beach." He smiled, then turned and walked back through the house.

After Barry left, Maddie decided that she would go have a look around town, but first she would take Bella and Polly for a walk along the beach. Just about everything in Bayview was centered around the large bay. Many houses were built around it, and the town's harbor was the hub of the businesses in the area. She strolled along the bay in the direction of the harbor, with her two dogs at her side. They kept an enthusiastic pace. She always found herself out of breath before they were.

As Maddie passed some familiar areas around the bay, she recalled the special moments she had spent there. There was where she'd had her first kiss with a boy who was only there for the summers. The bench ahead of her was where she'd spent the night when she'd run away from home, due to her mother insisting she eat an entire serving of green beans. She laughed at the memory, as now she knew that her mother could watch her the entire night from the house. She'd felt so brave the next day when she woke up, it never occurred to her that she'd never been in any danger. When her stomach rumbled, she'd decided the green beans weren't so bad, and plodded back home.

It was strange to lose herself in memories that hadn't crossed her mind in years. As she neared the harbor, she heard sounds that had once been part of her daily life. The calls of the fishermen as they reported their catches. The subtle clang of buoys in the water. The grind of the trucks as they backed boats into the water. She took a deep breath of the fresh air and felt transported through time. Was it possible that Bayview hadn't changed at all in the past thirty years? Growing up there had been a unique experience.

The small town fostered fierce loyalty among its residents. Most were very involved in local politics, sports, and the schools. She could recall the entire town turning out for her graduation, not because everyone had children graduating, but because the entire town considered the graduating class, part of their family. It had its perks and drawbacks. It meant she could walk into a store as a young girl and get a free sample of just about anything available. It also meant that when she had that first kiss by the bay, the entire town knew about it within the hour. She laughed to herself as the memories continued to flood her mind.

Maddie walked back toward home. The dogs had been on a long trip that day and every new smell and sound made them excited, she was sure they could use a rest. After making sure they had everything they needed, she hopped in her car to drive to town.

Maddie started down the main road that led along the harbor. Right on the corner, as expected, stood Harver's Surf Shop. It had been there as long as she could remember. She smiled at the sight of it, but her smile faded as she noticed a closed sign in its window. She wondered if it might have been closed just for the day. As she neared her favorite restaurant, she was relieved to see that it was still open. When she lived there, it was the only restaurant in town and it looked as if it still was.

Janet's Place was part café, part diner, and part Italian restaurant, as if she couldn't decide which she liked better. It became the central meeting place for most people in the town not long after it opened, when

Maddie was a teen. She pulled open the door, eager to have a chat with Janet and order a chocolate milkshake. Lately, she had been trying to eat healthier, but she decided one milkshake wouldn't hurt. Janet's made the best shakes.

The young girl at the front counter looked up from her phone with a forced smile.

"What can I get you?"

Maddie slid into a stool at the counter and smiled in return.

"A chocolate shake, please, extra thick."

"Extra thick?" She blinked.

"Yes, extra thick." Maddie raised an eyebrow. "Don't you still serve milkshakes here?"

"Yes. But I don't know how to make it extra thick." She lowered her phone. "Is that some kind of joke or something?"

"What's going on here?" A tall woman, who looked to be in her seventies, walked up to the counter. "Is there a problem, Lacy?"

"This lady wants an extra thick milkshake." Lacy quickly tucked her phone in her pocket.

"Extra thick, huh?" The woman swung around to face Maddie. "My word! Is it really you?" Her eyes lit up at the sight of her.

"Janet?" Maddie stared into the woman's familiar features. She had to dig a bit past the wrinkles, and the different hairstyle, but she could still see Janet, the no-nonsense owner of the restaurant.

"Maddie!" Janet laughed as she clapped her hands in one sharp snap. "I didn't think I'd live to see the day that you came back here!"

"Here I am." Maddie grinned. "But apparently, you don't serve extra thick milkshakes anymore?"

"No one ever asks for them!" Janet placed one hand on her hip and rolled her eyes. "Now, they just want to know the calorie content and whether the milk is organic. Don't worry, I'll fix you right up." She walked over to the blender. "I can't believe you're here! I really thought that old house would be up for sale soon." She glanced over her shoulder. "Is that why you're here? To sell it?"

"No, I'm here to stay." Maddie forced a smile as she remembered trying to discuss selling the house with Craig as part of their retirement plan.

Now, she understood why he always avoided the topic. She had inherited her mother's house along with her sister and Maddie had wanted to sell it and use her share of the money toward buying a small house in the country they could eventually retire in. But he always made excuses. Now, she knew that there wasn't any money to buy the house. Even after selling everything she owned, including the house he'd taken a second mortgage out on, she didn't have enough money to live on. She had a few freelance bookkeeping jobs, but not nearly enough to support herself.

It was either move back to Bayview or move in with one of her children. She didn't want to add a burden to their budding lives. And she needed her space as well. Not to mention they would also have to take in Bella and Polly. The truth was, if she couldn't find some way to earn more money, she might still be forced to turn to one of her children.

"I'm glad to hear that." Janet gave her hand a light pat. "You'll settle back in just fine, Maddie. We'll all be happy to have you. Now, let me get you that extra thick chocolate milkshake." She grinned as she turned away to prepare the shake.

"Extra thick chocolate milkshake!" A voice squealed from a few steps behind Maddie. "I knew I'd find you here!"

CHAPTER 3

*M*addie spun around on the stool and smiled into the familiar features of her friend, Amber. Although her features had aged over the years, she still looked the same to Maddie. Maybe it was because of the sparkle in her eye, or the shock of blonde hair that snaked its way through the gray bun piled on top of her head, but whatever it was, she recognized her right away.

"Amber!" Maddie spread her arms wide as she stood up from the stool.

"Maddie!" Amber's slender arms wrapped around her and squeezed tight.

Maddie struggled to take a breath for a moment, then laughed. Amber had always been a bear-hugger. As she took a step back to look Amber over, she noticed that her friend was as fit as ever. She always had a new fitness passion when they were younger, everything from cross-country running, to yoga, and it seemed that hadn't changed. "It's so great to see you, Amber." She sighed as she gazed at her friend. "I don't know why I let so many years slip by."

"Shh, don't worry about that." Amber cupped her cheeks and smiled. "All that matters is we're here now. I was so excited when I heard you were coming back. I just hope that you're really here to stay."

"So far, it looks that way." Maddie shrugged as the weight of her reason for moving to Bayview settled on her shoulders. "I don't really have any other choice."

"Well, I for one, am glad the universe has swept you back into my world." Amber ordered a smoothie from the waitress, then turned her attention back to Maddie. "Honestly, how are you still this gorgeous?"

"Gorgeous?" Maddie gave a short laugh. "Which part? The wrinkles or the extra pounds?"

"Stop it. You have always been gorgeous and you know it. Look at all of that wavy, black hair, and those bright blue eyes, and your figure." Amber sighed, then clucked her tongue. "You really shouldn't hide it in such plain clothes."

"Alright, alright, enough of the flattery." Maddie laughed. "Please, I'm enjoying my milkshake."

"As you should." Amber settled on the stool beside Maddie's and took her smoothie from the waitress. "Thanks so much, Lacy. This looks perfect."

"I added some extra blueberries." Lacy grinned at her.

"Oh, I guess that means I'll be adding an extra tip." Amber winked at her. "Oh, could you pack me up two of those muffins, the ones with the cranberries in them. I want to take them home to Mom."

"Sure, I'll get them for you." Lacy stepped into the kitchen.

"Speaking of your mother, how is she?" Maddie felt some relief to have the chance to gab with her friend. Despite them not being in touch much over the years, she felt as if no time had passed when Amber slung her arm around her shoulders.

"As feisty as ever." Amber rolled her eyes. "I can't get her to slow down, and trust me, I've tried. Every time a doctor says she needs to start taking it easy, she fires him on the spot, and walks out."

"Ah, just like I remember her." Maddie grinned as she sipped her milkshake. "I can't wait to see her."

"Oh, I'm sure you won't be waiting long. She's looking forward to seeing you."

"I'm so glad I ran into you. I was really starting to wonder if I could get used to being back here, but seeing you again makes me remember all of the good times." Maddie lowered her voice as she looked down at the countertop. "Amber, I'm sorry for not keeping in touch more."

"Sweetheart, you've had your own life to live. So have I, it doesn't mean we love each other any less." Amber met her eyes. "I knew when your mother passed that you would never want to come back here.

I know that you don't want to be here now. So, why don't you tell me the truth? Why are you really back here, Maddie? What's gone wrong?"

Amber always had a way of cutting right to the point.

"It wasn't what I planned on, that's for sure." Maddie nodded. "Let's just say, my husband had a few secrets, and now we're divorced."

"Let's say more than that." Amber put her hand over hers. "I want to hear all of it. Every detail." She squeezed her hand. "And I'm very sorry for what's happened, Maddie. I know how much you loved him, at least at some point. I heard it in your voice every time you talked about him."

"I did love him." Maddie took a deep breath. "And I still do in a way. Despite, everything." She waved her hand. "I don't even know how to begin to explain it, other than to say, I found out that just about everything in my life was a lie."

"Not everything, I'm sure." Amber looked into her eyes. "You have three beautiful children, that much I know is real."

"And a granddaughter now, too." Maddie smiled at the thought, then nodded. "You're right, not everything was a lie. But I can't help feeling like a fool. I thought I knew my husband, but he had been keeping so many secrets from me. He was so deceitful. And now his deceit has landed him behind bars."

"I'm sorry that he betrayed you. But maybe all of

that can be behind you now." Amber scooted closer to her. "You have a chance for a fresh start. After all you've been through, it could be a really good thing."

"You think?" Maddie smiled some as she gazed at her friend. "I hadn't really considered that."

"Sure. You can fix up the house exactly the way you like it, you can set your own schedule now, you get to do whatever you want." Amber gave her shoulder a shove. "Everything is up to you!"

"You always have a way of cheering me up." Maddie laughed as she leaned close to hug her. "How, after all of these years, do you still have that talent?"

"You must bring it out in me." Amber grinned. "I'm just happy that we can be together again. It doesn't matter how many years have passed, you're still the same Maddie, and I'm still the same Amber."

"I'm so glad we are." Maddie released a sigh of relief. She'd been nervous about returning to Bayview after so many years. Although, it welcomed its own, it wasn't known for being too friendly to outsiders. She didn't know what she would be to her hometown, a member of the community returning home, or a stranger that had been gone too long. So far, she'd felt nothing but welcomed.

"Amber! Oh, Amber!" A woman waved from a few tables away, then stood up and walked toward them.

"Hi Nancy, how are you today?" Amber smiled at her. "Nancy, this is my friend, Maddie. Maddie, this is

Nancy. She bought the little bungalow on the south side of the bay with her husband, Max."

"Nice to meet you, Maddie." Nancy cleared her throat, then looked at Amber. "Have you seen Helen?" She glanced around the restaurant nervously.

"Helen? No." Amber frowned as she studied the younger woman. "Why? Is something wrong?"

"Oh, it's nothing, I'm sure. I just want to try smooth things over after the disagreement we had at the town meeting, but I haven't been able to catch up with her." Nancy sighed. "She hasn't been a fan of mine since the last meeting." She wrung her hands. "I never should have spoken up like I did, I know better than that."

"I liked what you had to say, Nancy." Amber met her eyes. "I think it was very brave of you. Don't worry about Helen. She's more bark than bite."

"Say that to the last person she shut down." Nancy shuddered as she clutched her purse at her side. "If you see her, please don't tell her that I was looking for her. She's obviously trying to avoid me. I don't want to upset her more than I already have. I think it's better if I just pretend that I just happened to run into her."

"Don't worry, I won't tell her, Nancy. But I'm sure everything is going to be fine." Amber watched as Nancy made her way out of the restaurant.

"What was all that about?" Maddie frowned as she noticed the strain in Amber's features.

"Ugh, Helen." Amber rolled her eyes. "Bayview's very own queen bee."

"Queen bee?" Maddie raised her eyebrows. "I don't remember any Helens, actually."

"She's not from here, she's an outsider. She married Chuck. Remember him?" Amber smiled some.

"Chuck! Of course! He was a couple of years younger than us, but we always let him hang out with us in the neighborhood. Remember when we tried to build that rocket ship together when we were kids?" Maddie smiled. "Oh, I'd love to see him again."

"Oh, you haven't heard?" Amber's smile faded.

"Heard what?" Maddie braced herself as she could already sense from Amber's tone it was bad news.

"Chuck had a heart attack about six months ago. It was sudden." Amber sighed.

"Oh no, I'm so sorry, that's terrible." Maddie realized there was a lot she had missed out on.

"He had a heart problem, but he was on medication for it. He had been fine since he started the medication, and had been pretty healthy aside from that, as far as we all knew. Ever since then, Helen has been on even more of a warpath." Amber frowned. "I think he managed to keep her calmer than anyone else could, now with him gone, she's just terrorizing the town."

"I don't understand, what exactly is she doing?" Maddie took the last sip of her milkshake.

"She's so bossy. She thinks she gets to make every

decision in the town. She came from a fairly wealthy family, in an elite suburb, and I think coming here was a huge step down for her. So, she's been trying to turn it into something it's not. She has had a big hand in getting all of these grants and business incentives. She insisted on the marina being expanded. Her latest venture is trying to get a luxury resort built here. Can you imagine, a luxury resort in Bayview?" Amber rolled her eyes as she laughed. "Those rich people would be run out of town."

"Very quickly. Although, the improvements might be good for the town." Maddie nodded as she narrowed her eyes. "But I'm sure she can't have that much influence around here."

"She does, actually. She's made friends with all of the right people, and now no one wants to cross her. What she says goes, most of the time, and she makes sure that she's heard. She's so loud, and determined, she'll take over an entire meeting, if she has to, but most of the time people don't even speak up." Amber sighed as she sat back in her chair. "When she wants something, there's no stopping her."

"She sounds like quite a force." Maddie pushed her empty glass away from her. "She sounds like someone I'd like to get to know."

"A force isn't exactly the word I'd use to describe her." Amber raised her eyebrows. "And you might regret that last statement, because here she comes."

CHAPTER 4

*A*mber took a deep breath as the door to the restaurant swung open and a woman dressed in a peach and hot pink, layered slip dress sashayed into the dining space.

"Oh wow." Maddie looked her over as a faint laugh bubbled up within her. "She knows how to make an entrance, doesn't she? I love the colors on that dress."

"She's always dressed in the fanciest clothes." Amber rolled her eyes. "She thinks it's best to always present yourself in the finest clothes you own."

"Interesting. I'm not sure how well that goes over in this town." Maddie settled her gaze on Helen.

"It didn't go over at all, at first. But since she's wormed her way in here, now the women turn to her for fashion advice, and the men do everything they can to impress her." Amber shook her head. "It's kind of ridiculous to watch, actually."

"I'm sure it is." Maddie narrowed her eyes.

"Oh, Amber, dear!" Helen waved to her as she walked toward their table. "I've been looking all over for you!"

"For me?" Amber's eyes widened. "Whatever for?"

"I heard that you used to be friends with that Maddie woman." Helen pursed her lips. "The one that owns that atrocity of a house near the bay with her sister. Rumor is that she's coming back to town, and when she arrives, I want you to tell me right away. I can't wait to speak to her about the mess they've let that house become. They have just let it rot away. Really!"

"Uh." Amber looked at Maddie, then back at Helen. "Well, the house isn't that bad, Helen. I think you're overreacting a bit."

"Not in the least!" Helen huffed. "It's an absolute shame what they have allowed it to become!"

"They just let it rot away, huh?" Maddie met the other woman's eyes as she smiled. "What terrible people."

"Absolutely awful." Helen clucked her tongue. "That house was once a shining star on the bay, now every time I have to look at it, well it just makes me sick."

"So sorry to hear that." Maddie shook her head.

"Life can get busy sometimes. Maybe they just haven't had a chance to come here and clean it up."

"Not so busy that a gem like that is allowed to fall into shambles." Helen crossed her arms, then tilted her head to the side. "Who are you? I don't believe we've ever met."

"Forgive my rudeness." Maddie held her hand out to greet her. "I'm that Maddie woman. It's nice to meet you, Helen."

"Oh, don't think that you've embarrassed me." Helen laughed as she snatched her hand back. "Not one bit! I stand by everything I just said. You need to get that house cleaned up and pristine or you'll be hearing from town hall."

"I'd love some advice on what you think needs to be done." Maddie leaned back in her chair as she spoke in a sweet tone. "It sounds like you know it better than me, even though I am the one who grew up in it."

"I have seen many pictures." Helen shrugged. "If we're going to get a luxury resort built in this town, our homes need to look the part, otherwise no one is going to want to vacation here."

"Or, we could go with the more realistic idea of the amusement park, which will draw visitors without destroying our natural surroundings." Amber rested her chin on her palm as she smiled at her. "That's an option, too, isn't it?"

"Alright ladies, I won't have any debates here."

Janet walked up to them with her hands on her hips. "Save that for the meetings."

"Quite alright, I'll just be on my way." Helen quirked an eyebrow as she looked at Maddie. "I do hope that you're going to get started on that house right away."

"Sure, of course." Maddie tried not to think about the balance in her checking account. If there were any major repairs, they were going to have to wait. She hoped that the house just needed a good clean and maybe a coat of paint. Hopefully, that would be enough to make Helen happy.

"Sorry, about that." Amber rolled her eyes. "Like I said, she's a pain."

"At least she's trying to do some good for the community. That's something, right?" Maddie stood up from the counter. "And she's right. I have let the house go. I should never have stayed away for so long."

"Anything I can do to help, just let me know." Amber hugged her, then looked into her eyes. "I'm so glad you're back, Maddie."

"Me too." Maddie smiled as she felt a sense of joy at returning home for the first time. Perhaps there was more to moving back to Bayview than she had first thought.

As Maddie drove back to her house, she noticed the places where she and Chuck would play. It was hard to believe he was gone.

She parked in her driveway and heard the excited barks of her girls through the window. She greeted them with warm hugs and stroked their fur. They had been her comfort since Craig had begun acting so strangely. Now, they were her comfort as she settled into her new life. She let them out in the yard to play and took a kitchen chair out to the front porch to relax for a while.

As the afternoon sun began to get lower in the sky, Maddie's attention was drawn to the water that stretched out before her. The bay had always been the pride of Bayview. It was the ultimate source of recreation, and beauty. She doubted there was a single home in Bayview that didn't have a picture of the sun setting over the bay somewhere in it.

But as Maddie looked out over the water, she noticed something strange at the water's edge. Although the bay often had branches floating in it, due to the high winds that often accompanied storms in the area, this wasn't a branch. It was brightly colored, and too big to be a child's toy. Startled by the sight of it, she decided to have a closer look.

Once Bella and Polly were safely inside the house, she made her way down the path that led to the water. Maybe it was a decoration from one of the stores in town that had blown off into the water. Perhaps something off one of the fishing boats in the harbor.

As Maddie drew closer, the object began to take shape. The shape left her unsettled to the core. It couldn't be, could it? Maybe one of the local kids had decided to play a prank of some kind. It happened, as kids could easily get bored in the small town. There still wasn't a lot for them to do. As she reached the edge of the water, her heart sank. What she had hoped was a prank, now looked very real. The brightly colored garment that wrapped around what appeared to be a body, shielded the face from view. Her breath caught in her throat as she recognized the color. It was the very dress that she noticed earlier in the day, the dress that Helen had been wearing.

A scream formed in the back of her throat, but she didn't have the strength to produce it. She crouched down beside the water and reached for the piece of cloth that covered what she hoped wasn't Helen's face. As she tugged it back and saw Helen's dead body, the scream that she'd felt too weak a second before to release, burst forth from her with its own strength. It carried across the water and echoed into the town.

Within seconds, neighbors from around the bay began to emerge from their homes. As Maddie's scream faded, she was aware that all eyes were on her, but it didn't occur to her to step away, or to ask for help. Instead, she reached into the water and pulled Helen's body farther onto the sandy shore. She could tell that there was no life left in the woman, but she still had to try to do something to help her.

Maddie was about to start chest compressions, when she heard a loud voice from just behind her.

"Don't touch her! Back away right now!"

The command in his tone made Maddie jump back from Helen's body. She spun around to find a man in a police uniform a few steps away from her. The sun glistened off the badge on his chest. His eyes were wide, and his graying hair was ruffled by the breeze that carried off the bay.

She vaguely heard him introduce himself as the police chief.

"Did you pull her out of the water?" He crouched down beside Helen's body and felt for any sign of a pulse.

"Yes." Maddie's voice wavered as she took another step away from Helen. "I just found Helen there. I wasn't sure what to do. I thought maybe there was a chance that she could be saved."

"No, it's far too late for that." He winced as he looked Helen over. He pulled his radio from his belt and spoke into it, then he looked up at Maddie. "You're going to need to tell me everything you saw, and everything you did, right from the first moment you saw Helen in the water."

"I didn't know it was her. Not right away." Maddie clasped her hands together as she tried to slow her breathing. "I saw something in the water from my porch, but I didn't think it was a person. I just thought it was a toy, or something." She drew a sharp breath. "I came down here to investigate. When I got close, I thought maybe it was just a prank." She shook her head. "But it wasn't."

"No, it wasn't." The police chief narrowed his eyes. "And that is when you should have called the police, instead of pulling the body out of the water."

"I'm sorry." Maddie's voice wavered. "I just thought, maybe I could help her. I just wanted to try."

His expression softened as he gazed at her. "It's alright." He stood up and walked toward her. "I'm sure this was quite a shock to you." He took a notepad out of his pocket. "Just take a minute, alright? But then I'm going to need to know everything. You're my best resource for answers about this right now."

"She must have drowned." Maddie was grateful that his tone had softened, and he seemed interested in comforting her.

"No, she didn't just drown." The police chief glanced at the body. "She was strangled." He looked back at Maddie and narrowed his eyes. "This was no accident."

CHAPTER 5

"*I*t's very important for you to remember every detail. Every sound that you heard. Anything that might stand out to you." The chief met Maddie's eyes.

"I told you everything already." Maddie couldn't believe that Helen had been murdered. "How could this happen?"

"You didn't tell me everything." The chief stepped closer to her. "I need you to focus. Listen to the sound of my voice."

Still shaken, but willing to try, Maddie closed her eyes and tried to focus on the sound of his voice.

"You're safe now." The chief's words settled all around her senses, both soothing and protective in the same moment. It was as if he was making her a promise. Her eyes fluttered back open and she stared into his eyes. Why did he seem so familiar to her? "Tell me, did you hear anything from your porch? Anything unusual? Maybe people arguing, water splashing, or even something like a scream?"

Maddie took a slow breath and did her best to remember. Then she shook her head. "I was watching my girls in the front yard, then I looked out over the water."

"Your girls? Were there other witnesses?" The chief's eyes narrowed.

"No, not exactly. They're my dogs." Maddie smiled slightly. "I didn't hear anything strange."

"But for some reason you looked at the water?" The chief raised an eyebrow. "What drew your attention? What made you look in that direction?"

"Just habit, I guess." Maddie sighed. "I always found comfort in the sight of the bay when I was growing up. I didn't look for any other reason. I just wanted to relax and watch it for a while."

"And when you did look, did you spot her right away?" The chief jotted down a note on his pad.

"I spotted something bright, something pink." Maddie realized that she had actually recognized the color as soon as she saw it. "It reminded me of the dress she'd been wearing earlier in the day. Maybe that was why I was so curious about what it was."

"So, you saw her earlier today?" He made another note. "Did you notice anything strange about her then?"

"It was the first time I'd met her. I was at Janet's at

around eleven." Maddie did her best not to look in the direction of Helen's body. "I don't really know anything about her. Other than what my friend, Amber, told me."

"Amber was there, too?" The chief lowered his notepad. "Who else? Did anyone else talk to Helen?"

"No, not that I saw. Oh, there was a woman looking for her before she came in, though. I think her name was Nancy." Maddie ran her hands across her face. "I'm sorry, I don't know anything."

"Just try to relax." The chief waited until she looked back up at him. "I need you to stay with me, alright? You're the one who might have the answers I need."

"I don't." Maddie took a step back. "I'm sorry, but I don't. I just arrived back in town. I didn't hear or see anything. I just found her like this." Her hands trembled as she shoved them into her pockets. "I didn't mean to cause any trouble by pulling her out of the water. I just hoped that I could save her."

"It's alright." The chief nodded as he studied her. "But sometimes you can know something, without realizing it. Sometimes things just stick with you, even if you aren't aware of them. You say that Nancy was looking for her? Did the two talk?"

"No, she left before Helen came in. She'd asked Amber not to tell Helen she was looking for her." Maddie took another deep breath. "I don't know anything, like I said."

"You know that she was wearing the same dress earlier. You know that she spoke to Amber. Those are things I didn't know. You say Amber and Nancy were afraid of Helen finding out that Nancy was looking for her?"

"I didn't say that. I didn't say that Amber was afraid." Maddie frowned. "I never said that at all."

"So, Amber was happy to see Helen?" The chief tipped his chin upward some as he looked down at her.

"Amber has nothing to do with any of this." Maddie crossed her arms. "I don't see how any of these questions are going to help your investigation. I'd really like to go back to my house now."

"Take this." The chief handed her his card. "This has my information on it. If you think of anything, please contact me." He handed her a slip of paper from his notepad. "Write down your name, address, and phone number for me, so I can get in contact with you. We can settle up the paperwork at another time."

"Thank you." Maddie put the card in her pocket and took the paper.

"Need a pen?" He pulled one out of his shirt pocket and offered it to her.

As Maddie took the pen from him, her fingertips brushed against his hand. She felt another rush of familiarity.

Maddie's hand still trembled as she wrote down

the information for him. When she handed it over, she met his eyes again.

"I do want to help in any way that I can. But there's nothing more that I can tell you."

"Is there someone I can call for you? To stay with you?" The chief paused for a moment, then spoke up again. "Your husband?"

"No, I'll be fine. Thanks." Maddie turned and walked back up to her house. Her heart still pounded against her chest. A part of her felt as if it had all been a dream and she hadn't seen what she thought she'd seen. As she reached the porch, she turned back to look down at the water again. Had she known it was Helen the whole time? Had some part of her suspected it from the first sighting of that shade of pink?

"Maddie!" Amber's shrill voice carried across the front yard as she rushed up to the porch. "I just heard! Are you okay?" She climbed up the steps and threw her arms around her.

"I'm okay." Maddie took a deep breath as she hugged her back. "What a crazy afternoon." She shook her head. "I never expected anything like this to happen."

"None of us did." With one arm still around Maddie's shoulders, Amber looked back at the water, where the police were still gathered. "It really is Helen?"

"Yes." Maddie nodded. "I'm so sorry for your loss."

"Thank you." Amber shook her head. "I don't think it's as much a loss as it is a shock. I just can't believe that she's gone." She pulled away and walked to the edge of the porch. "Was it an accident?"

"I believe the chief thinks it was murder." Maddie wrapped her arms around herself to stay warm as another chilly breeze carried across the water. "I'm not sure exactly what he thinks, though. He's hard to read."

"He always has been, hasn't he?" Amber glanced back at her.

"I'm not sure I know what you mean." Maddie stepped up beside her.

"Never mind, I guess it doesn't matter, now." Amber leaned against the porch railing. "This town is going to be in chaos by tomorrow morning. Helen had her hands in everything. Every business is going to be affected."

"And what about Chuck's poor mother? Beatrice?" Maddie clasped her hands together. "She'll be so heartbroken. First her son, and now her daughter-in-law. I'm guessing she never remarried?"

"No, she's been alone all of this time. Beatrice and Chuck stayed very close. She was almost always at the shop with him." Amber lowered her voice. "To be honest, I didn't think she was going to survive his death. But somehow she managed to keep going. At least she has her sister, Shirley. She has spent a lot of time with her helping her out. Keeping her company."

Maddie didn't know Shirley very well, but she was often at Beatrice's house when she was growing up. She was a teacher at the local school but never taught Maddie's class. Maddie remembered that she had lost her daughter, who was only a teen at the time, due to a heart condition. Shirley got divorced soon after. After she lost her daughter, she would spend a lot of time with Beatrice.

"I noticed that the surf shop was closed when I drove into town. Do you know anything about that? I don't think I've ever seen it closed during the day." Maddie watched as a few of the police cars drove away.

"Helen shut it down not long after Chuck died. She hadn't reopened it. People mostly assumed it was because she needed time to grieve for the loss of her husband, but I'm not so sure."

"What do you think?" Maddie nudged her friend's shoulder with her own. "What's the real story?"

"I can't say for sure, but as far as I know she never really liked the shop. She's always had big aspirations, and she saw that place as tiny. Chuck loved it, though. He would spend most of his time there. I still don't know how those two ever got along. They were like total opposites, but Chuck never seemed to mind."

"You never heard them argue?" Maddie raised an eyebrow.

"I'm sure they did, but no I'd never heard them myself." Amber shook her head.

"Do you want to come in for some tea? You can meet my babies." Maddie smiled. "They always cheer me up."

"Babies?" Amber grinned.

CHAPTER 6

*N*ot long after Maddie introduced Amber to Bella and Polly, the police lights by the bay disappeared. Maddie looked out through the window at the space where they had once been. Was that it? Did Helen's death simply vanish from the idyllic bayside view? She was curious to find out what had happened to her. With her heart still racing, she turned back to Amber, and the two dogs that claimed her lap.

"You should know that I did mention to the police that we spoke to Helen earlier." Maddie sat down on the couch beside her. "Just in case they ask you questions."

"Oh, I'm not worried about the local police." Amber shrugged. "I just hope they can get to the bottom of this. The town was just starting to get back on its feet, something like this could really derail all of those plans."

"Helen was such a big part of those changes. I wonder if that's why someone targeted her?" Maddie frowned as she sat back against the couch. "Someone must know something about what happened."

"If there's anyone that knows everything about this town, it would be Chuck's mother, Beatrice. I'm sure she's heard about all of this by now."

"Poor woman is going to be grieving yet again." Maddie shook her head.

"I don't know about that." Amber ran her hand over the dogs' backs. "I don't think she had much affection for Helen. In fact, as I recall, she didn't even attend the wedding."

"Really? She didn't attend her only child's wedding?" Maddie's eyes widened. "What could have happened that made her that angry?"

"I'm not sure, but things didn't thaw out over the years, as far as I could tell." Amber gave the dogs a few more pets. "I should be going, I don't like to leave my mother alone for too long at night." The dogs jumped off her lap as she stood up.

"Your mother." Maddie smiled as she stood up as well. "I can't wait to see her."

"We'll have to get together tomorrow." Amber hugged her. "I'm sorry that all of this happened, but I am glad to have you back."

"Thanks, Amber." Maddie walked her to the door, with Bella and Polly at her side. Once she closed the door, she felt the events of the day hit her with a wave of tiredness. "Alright girls, let's find somewhere to sleep." She headed up the stairs to her old room. Inside, she found her bed covered in a white sheet. She pulled the sheet off to reveal it exactly as she'd left it. "Well, it might be a little dusty, but it'll be soft." She sprawled out across it, and Bella and Polly curled up on either side of her. "We'll get it all washed tomorrow."

When the sun broke through the curtain the next morning, Maddie woke to soft dog snores, as the memories of the previous day flooded her mind. None of it had been a dream. Helen really was dead.

After taking the dogs for a walk and stopping at the grocery store, she returned determined to find out at least a little more about the woman she'd pulled out of the water.

Maddie prepared one of her mother's favorite comfort foods, anything with chocolate. In this case she was going to bake chocolate cupcakes. She loved baking, but she hadn't baked since Craig and her had separated, she just hadn't been in the mood, but she wanted to do something for Beatrice.

Maddie's kids loved her cupcakes. She would come up with new flavor combinations for them to try. But the chocolate cupcakes were their favorite. Whenever she baked, it brought her a sense of peace. She'd seen her mother take baked treats to home after home as she was growing up. Whenever someone was ill, or there had been a loss, she would head straight over with something. Despite having a bakery to run, she always made time for her friends.

Maddie thought about baking in her own kitchen for her children. The thought made her smile. She remembered the summers that her niece, Katie, would come to visit and they would spend hours baking together. They had become very close during that time.

Maddie loved baking as a hobby, and although her sister, Tammy, enjoyed baking, Tammy's daughter, Katie, had the real talent and passion for it. She had definitely inherited it from her grandmother and ever since she was old enough she would take any chance she could get to bake with her. She had recently graduated from pastry school and was working at a bakery.

Maddie put the cupcakes in a container, saving a few in case she got any visitors, then started toward the door. Her two dogs began to follow her.

"No, no, you're going to have to stay here for this visit." Maddie shooed them back away from the door. "I won't be long." She blew them kisses, then headed out the door.

As Maddie drove in the direction of Beatrice's house, she marveled at just how much the same everything looked to her. Despite some modern updates, the buildings still remained, and though some of the stores had changed names, they still looked familiar. The park on the corner still had the same stone benches, and chess tables. The streetlights were wrapped in sparkling stars as they had been when she was a young girl. The town took pride in its image, and she guessed that Helen had amplified that more than ever. How would it survive her death? Her murder?

Maddie recalled the Chuck she'd known as a young girl. He was always doing something to torment her and Amber. He would throw mud balls at them or push them into the water. But if anyone looked at them funny, he would go into protection mode. Even if his opponents were twice his size. He never allowed anyone to do anything to harm them. When she'd graduated from high school and was about to move away, he'd given her a big hug, and made her promise not to forget him. She hadn't. But she hadn't made any effort to reconnect with him, either.

Maddie recalled how life had swept her up into a sense of busyness that seemed to never stop. Until it had all come crashing down around her. Now, she wished she'd taken the time to reach out to him. She hadn't even heard when he got married. She wondered how he had ended up with someone like Helen. She was so stern, so loud. Did he like that about her? Did he think that she would protect him the way that he had always tried to protect others?

Maddie parked in the long driveway of Beatrice's

home. It was the same driveway she had run up and down many times as a kid, playing tag with Amber and Chuck. It led up to Beatrice's three-story house. Chuck was from one of the wealthier families in the town but no one really paid attention to that when they were kids. He had the nicer swing set, and his own pool to swim in, but he was still just another kid in the neighborhood.

Maddie looked up at the bay window of the house and wondered if Beatrice would even remember her. It had been so long since the last time they spoke. How could she apologize for missing her son's funeral? She hadn't even known that he'd died to offer her condolences. Now the woman was even more alone, with her daughter-in-law gone as well.

She walked up to the front door and knocked on it.

"Maddie! Maddie, get in here this instant!" Beatrice threw the door open, then opened her arms wide for Maddie.

"Hi, Bea." Maddie smiled as she wrapped her arms around her in a warm hug.

"Where have you been?" Beatrice cupped Maddie's cheeks. "All these years have gone by, and look at you, just as young and fresh-faced as I remember!"

"Bea, where are your glasses?" Maddie laughed as Beatrice took the cupcakes from her.

"Ah, you have no idea how much I've missed this. Your mother's recipe?" Beatrice breathed in the scent of them as she carried them toward the kitchen.

"Bea." A woman called from the steps as she came down them. "Oh, sorry, I didn't know someone was here." She stopped at the bottom. Maddie noticed that she looked like Beatrice, she was also tall, but thinner than her and a few years younger.

"Shirley." Beatrice turned toward the woman. "You remember Maddie. Emma's daughter."

"Oh, yes of course." Shirley opened her arms as she walked over to Maddie to give her a hug. "I heard you were back. It's so nice to see you."

"And you." Maddie smiled as she hugged her in return. Maddie was pleased to see that Beatrice had some company.

"We must catch up some time." Shirley pulled away from her, then grabbed her purse by the counter. "But I'm sorry, I have to run. I have a hair appointment and I'm running late." She fluffed her short, brown curls with one hand.

"I'd love to catch up." Maddie nodded.

"I'll be back later, Bea." Shirley called over her shoulder as she headed toward the door.

As the door closed, Beatrice turned toward Maddie and placed the cupcakes on the counter.

"I don't know what I would do without Shirley." Beatrice smiled as she sighed.

"It is good to be close to your sister." Maddie also smiled as she thought of her own sister. Although sometimes they drifted apart as they lived in different states and led such different lives, they could always count on each other.

"You know, when my husband died, your mother baked me something every week for over a year. I gained twenty pounds, but I swear it gave me something to look forward to at a time when I wasn't sure that I'd make it."

"No, I didn't know that." Maddie paused at the entrance of the large kitchen. "Bea, I'm so sorry about Chuck. I didn't know, or I would have been here."

"Oh, don't worry about that." Beatrice set the cupcakes down on the island in the middle of the kitchen, then turned to face her. "Sweetheart, lives get busy, I know that."

"And now you've lost Helen, too." Maddie walked over to her and took her hand. "I'm sorry you've been faced with so much grief."

"It's life." Beatrice shrugged. "But death is always a surprise. Even when the doctors say it will happen, even when you're old and gray, it's still a surprise." She leaned against the island and for the first time the tall, broad woman, appeared frail. Maddie guessed she was in her early seventies, and though she appeared as determined as ever, she noticed some fraying around the edges of that strength. "I was in shock after Chuck died. Now, at least I can have some peace."

"What do you mean?" Maddie frowned as she

continued to hold her hand. "Doesn't it upset you that Helen is gone?"

"That girl." Beatrice gritted her teeth, then shook her head. "Life is precious, I know that. But don't expect me to shed a tear over her." She took a deep breath, then gestured to the cupcakes. "Let's eat and have some tea. I can't wait to hear about what's been happening in your life."

Startled by her disregard for Helen, she joined Beatrice at the kitchen table, but her thoughts traveled back to the woman in the pink and peach dress. Was there anyone in Bayview that would grieve her death?

CHAPTER 7

s Maddie drove away from Beatrice's house, memories of Chuck flooded her mind again. She regretted missing his funeral. Perhaps if she had stayed in touch better, she would have known about it. But would she have come back for it?

Maddie decided to honor Chuck in her own way. Maybe she hadn't attended the funeral, but that didn't mean she couldn't say goodbye. She headed for the local florist. Although it was in the same building that it always had been, she noticed that it had a new name in bold, green letters across the top.

"Flowers by Frances." She smiled at the sound of the name. "How clever." She parked in front of the shop, then stepped out of her car. The windows were filled with a wide assortment of flowers in all different colors. As she opened the door to the shop, the various

CINDY BELL

scents greeted her in the same moment that a young woman behind the counter did.

"Welcome to Flowers by Frances, can I help you find anything today?" She stepped out from behind the counter.

"Thank you, I'm just looking for a bouquet I think." Maddie looked over the bouquets lined up in coolers on one wall. Each one was beautiful. She had no idea how to narrow it down.

"Maybe if you could tell me the occasion, I could make a suggestion?" The woman stepped up beside her. "I'm Frances by the way."

"I'm Maddie." Maddie smiled as she looked over at her. "I appreciate your help." She looked back at the flowers. "I want something to leave on the grave of a friend of mine."

"Oh, I'm so sorry for your loss." Frances frowned. "We do have some beautiful sympathy arrangements."

"Actually, I think I want something a bit more cheerful." Maddie met Frances' eyes. "He was always so cheerful. Always playful and getting into trouble. Something with lots of yellows, and blues, for the sun and the bright blue sky. Yes, I think that would be nice."

"A lovely choice." Frances smiled. "I can put one together for you, if you don't mind waiting for a few minutes."

"No, I don't mind waiting at all. Thank you so much." Maddie continued to browse through the flowers as Frances arranged a bouquet of brightly colored flowers. She smiled to herself at the thought of what Chuck might say about her buying flowers.

"Flowers for me? I always knew you loved me, Maddie." He would grin, and then slap her hard on the back.

Maddie closed her eyes briefly as she remembered the sound of his voice. Had it changed since the last time she spoke to him? Had it aged? Was he still the same cheerful guy, or did being married to Helen alter that personality?

"What do you think?" Frances held up the bouquet she'd completed.

"This is perfect, thank you so much." Maddie handed over her credit card to pay for them.

"If you don't mind me asking, is your friend someone local?" Frances met her eyes.

"Yes, but I'm afraid I'm a bit late to be honoring his passing. I moved away and wasn't aware that he had passed on, until I came back here. His name was Chuck." Maddie smiled to herself. "And he was such a good friend to me when we were young."

"Helen's husband?" Frances' hand trembled as she handed back the credit card.

"Yes. Did you know him?" Maddie felt a rush of curiosity as she noticed the change in Frances' demeanor.

"I did. A little." Frances cleared her throat. "I think

he would love these flowers. It's a sweet thing you're doing."

"Thanks for your help." Maddie was tempted to ask more about her connection to Chuck, but the moment felt awkward. As she turned toward the door, it swung open, and a police officer stepped inside. She recognized him from the previous day, but she hadn't learned his name. As he strode toward the front counter, she read it from his name tag.

Cooper.

She started to push the door open to leave, when she heard the tone of his voice.

"Frances, I need to speak to you." He stopped in front of the counter.

Maddie decided to linger a moment longer, curious as to why he had charged inside with such a commanding attitude.

"What is it, Cooper?" Frances stared straight at him.

"I need to ask you some questions about your relationship with Helen." Cooper pulled a notepad out of his pocket.

"We didn't have a relationship." Frances crossed her arms as she studied him. "What is this about?"

"I think you know exactly what this is about." Cooper's tone grew even more stern. "I've heard from a few other people that you made threats against Helen and you were quite angry with her."

"We exchanged words." Frances' hands fell back

to her sides as her eyes widened. "Is this about Helen's death? You can't be serious! You think I'm involved?"

"I have to ask these questions. I expect you to answer them as truthfully as you can. Did you threaten Helen?" Cooper's pen hovered over the pad he held.

"Not like that." Frances huffed. "I would never do anything to hurt Helen. She knew that. You know it, too. This is ridiculous."

"Answer the questions, Frances. I don't want to take you down to the station." Cooper smacked the pad hard on the counter in front of her.

Frances jumped at the sound.

Maddie did, too. She took a sharp breath as she wondered just how agitated the officer would get. She certainly wasn't going to leave now, she wanted to hear what Frances had to say and make sure she was okay.

"Did you threaten her?" Cooper repeated.

"Yes, I threatened her. But everyone knows I was just angry. She was trying to destroy my business! She spread lies all over town about the quality of my flowers! I was losing customers because of her. Of course I was angry." Frances shook her head. "I can't believe that you would even consider me a suspect."

"When you threatened her, what exactly did you say?" Cooper stared hard into her eyes.

"I don't remember my exact words." Frances frowned and rubbed the back of her neck.

"Try!" Cooper demanded.

Maddie felt as if Cooper was being a bit too harsh with Frances and she immediately felt her protective motherly instinct to step in and help her.

"That's quite enough." Maddie stepped forward, her voice stronger than she expected it to be. "She doesn't actually have to answer any of your questions, and you know that."

"Do I?" Cooper spun around to face Maddie. "Do you know the consequences for interfering with a police investigation?"

"It's alright." Frances breathed a sigh of relief. "Please, don't get yourself into trouble over me."

"Oh, I'm not going to get into any trouble. All I am doing is ensuring Frances knows her rights." Maddie stared hard into the officer's eyes as years of pent up frustration flooded through her. She'd let Craig tell her what to do, she'd let him lie to her and insist that he knew best. But she wouldn't let anyone do that to her anymore. Her instincts told her that Frances needed her help, someone needed to stand up to Cooper, who Maddie felt was intimidating Frances.

"And just what is your name?" Cooper narrowed his eyes.

"Maddie. But that's not important. Isn't there a murder you're supposed to solve?" Maddie raised her eyebrows. "Do you think it's going to be solved arguing with me?"

"I think you should keep your nose out of police

business." Cooper glanced back at Frances, then turned and walked out of the shop.

"Wow." Frances stared after him, then turned her attention to Maddie. "I don't think I've ever seen anyone speak to him like that."

"I didn't like the way he was speaking to you." Maddie frowned. "I wanted to make sure you know your rights."

"Thank you, Maddie. But you don't have to worry about it." Frances shrugged. "It's the way Cooper is. He always gives people a hard time."

"Well, I think he could have been less harsh when he spoke to you. Thank you again for the flowers." Maddie met Frances' eyes. Though she was tempted to ask her more about her threat against Helen, she didn't want to push her and upset her. "I'm sure I'll be back soon to get some flowers for my house."

"So, you're here to stay?" Frances smiled.

"It looks that way." Maddie pushed the door open and stepped outside. All at once she felt like she was home again. Bayview hadn't been her home for a long time, but now it seemed as if she might never have left.

CHAPTER 8

addie decided she wanted to try and find out more about what was happening with the investigation. Maybe if she knew what was happening, she could help solve the murder and get the cops off Frances' back. The best person to speak to would be the person in charge. The local police chief. She had no idea if he would tell her anything, but it was worth a try. She realized that she had left the card he had given her in the pocket of her pants at home, so she dialed the number of the local police station as she stepped out of the florist. After a few rings, a cheerful voice answered.

"Bayview Police Department, how may I help you?"

"I'd like to speak to someone about a case. Is the police chief there?" Maddie walked over to her car and opened the door.

"Not at the moment. He should be back soon," the officer replied. "Can I get your name, please?"

"It's Maddie Mills." Maddie looked over at the bouquet of flowers on the passenger seat.

"I can jot down a message to give to Chief Holden, but he's not in right now." She paused.

"Wait, did you say Chief Holden?" Maddie narrowed her eyes. She knew a boy named Holden growing up, and as far as she knew he didn't have any brothers. She could vaguely remember him introducing himself when he approached her after she had discovered Helen's body, but she was in so much shock she wasn't concentrating on him. "Jake Holden?"

"Yes, of course. He's the chief." She laughed. "Ma'am, are you okay?"

"Yes, I'm fine, thank you. I just moved back to town and I wasn't familiar with who the chief is just yet." Maddie recalled Jake as a skinny boy that only liked to talk about space and superheroes. She couldn't picture him as the muscular man that she'd met yesterday. Was it possible that she remembered him wrong? "Can you please ask him to call me." She rattled off her number.

"I will."

"Thank you so much." Maddie ended the call, then stared out through the windshield. Jake Holden was the chief? Jake, who sat behind her in class and plucked at her hair, never hard enough to hurt her,

57

just hard enough to annoy her? The very thought made her laugh out loud.

Then again, maybe it made sense. He was always doing his best to be in charge. To boss people around. He would set the rules for any games they played. He would turn in anyone misbehaving to the teacher. She shook her head as she started her car. Yes, it all made sense now.

Why had he seemed strange toward her? Because she didn't remember him? Or maybe because he did remember her? She searched through her memories for any time she might have done something to upset him. She winced as she realized there were quite a few, not the least of which was the night of the Junior prom, when he had confiscated a bottle of beer from her purse on her way into the dance. She'd shouted at him for being nosy, and he'd shouted right back at her for breaking the rules.

"The rules are the rules to protect you, Maddie."

Maddie heard his voice ringing through her mind, just as clearly as it had on that night. She'd been furious. But when she'd actually thought about it, she'd admitted to herself that he might have been right. She might have not enjoyed the night as much, if she had been tipsy. Of course, she'd never tell him that. Not then, when he was just a skinny teen with a hero complex, and not now when he had apparently morphed into a totally different version of himself.

Instead, Maddie had told him to mind his own business, and never speak to her again. Was that the last thing she'd ever said to him? Her mind raced through a few other memories, but nothing stood out to her. She pushed the thoughts from her mind and focused instead on Chuck.

Maddie picked her way through the well-manicured grass that led up to his gravestone. The sight of it shocked her, almost as much as her father's had. Her heart fluttered at the sight of Chuck's name carved into it. She wanted to believe he was somewhere better, somewhere that he could hear her words.

"I'm sorry I wasn't here, Chuck. I'm sorry we didn't have the chance to share our memories. You were such a big part of everything that was wonderful about Bayview for me. I never should have stayed so far away for so long. But I'm back now, I've moved back. I got you these." Maddie placed the flowers down gently.

She gazed down at the flowers. The bright petals stood out against the gray surface. They did look cheerful, despite the circumstances. "I hope you like them." She bit into her bottom lip as she felt a bit ridiculous. Yet, it gave her some comfort to think that somewhere he was smiling. She almost expected the sunny, clear sky, to get crowded with rain clouds, just so that he could splash her one last time.

But the sun continued to shine, and not a drop of rain threatened.

"I might not have been the best friend to you, Chuck, but there is something I can do for you, now," Maddie whispered. "I will help find out who killed your wife."

As Maddie turned away from the grave, she felt a pang of guilt for moving so far away. She was relieved that her mother had moved in with her in her final years and she could spend that time with her before she had passed. She took another step and looked up just in time to see a gold badge on a broad chest.

"Oh my!" Maddie gasped as the person stepped back to avoid the collision.

"I didn't mean to startle you." The police chief frowned as he took another step back.

Maddie's eyes ran the length of his uniform, then settled on his eyes. Yes, she could see it now, the striking green that they had always been. Such big eyes, for such a small boy, she had thought more than once, while they were growing up. How hadn't she noticed them yesterday?

"You did." Maddie waited for her heart to stop pounding as she continued to stare at him.

"I'm sorry. I thought it was best not to interrupt." Jake gestured toward Chuck's grave.

Maddie recalled the way he'd pushed her about Helen yesterday. She thought about the officer he had likely trained, and the way that officer spoke to Frances. Maybe his body had changed quite a bit, but his desire to be in charge likely hadn't. She braced herself for what might come next.

CHAPTER 9

addie reminded herself to think things through before she said anything. She'd always been one to speak her mind, and never be held back by anyone. That didn't always translate well when dealing with law enforcement.

"It wasn't my intention to disturb you." Jake's jaw locked briefly, then relaxed again as he took a breath.

"What are you doing here?" Maddie stared at him, still stunned by the idea that he could be the same lanky boy that would toy with her hair.

"I heard that you wanted to speak to me." Jake pulled his hat off and held it in front of him as he gazed at the gravestone just past her. "I noticed your car in the parking lot as I drove past. I thought I'd speak to you in person to find out what you wanted."

"I wanted to see what was happening with the

case. If there were any new developments." Maddie locked her eyes to his.

"I can't really tell you much." Jake shook his head.

"I understand." Maddie continued to marvel over her memories of him. Had he really grown into this self-assured, strong man? "I witnessed Officer Cooper interviewing Frances from Flowers by Frances and I thought that he could have been a bit gentler. She seemed upset by his questions."

Maddie raised her eyebrows as she braced herself for the possibility that he believed his officer had been in the right.

"I'll speak to him." Jake took a step toward her.

"Thank you." Maddie breathed a sigh of relief. "Do you remember me, Jake?"

Jake gazed at her for a long moment, as if he wasn't sure how to respond, then nodded.

"Of course, I remember you, Maddie."

So, he hadn't forgotten her. Yet, he treated her like a complete stranger. Had they become that over the years? As memories flooded her mind, it felt like just yesterday that she'd shooed him away, but the reality was, it had been decades.

"Why didn't you say anything yesterday?"

"You didn't say anything, either." Jake shrugged as he glanced away from her. "I just assumed you wanted to keep things professional."

"Jake, I just didn't recognize you." Maddie smiled some. "You've changed so much. It's hard for me to believe so many years have passed. You look fantastic."

"Thank you, so do you." Jake returned her smile. "It is astounding how fast the time goes by, isn't it?"

"Yes." Maddie's mind spun briefly through the lifetime she'd lived since she left Bayview. "You've done so well for yourself, Jake. I'm so happy to see that life has been good."

"It's had its moments." Jake flipped his hat in a slow circle as he studied her. "And how has life treated you?"

Maddie hesitated to answer. How could she? He'd become the chief, and her life had fallen apart. She doubted that he wanted to hear about that. He'd followed the rules and become successful, and she had, as he'd once warned she would, stumbled into a whole lot of trouble.

"It's had its moments." Maddie glanced over her shoulder at the flowers she'd placed. "So much has changed here, and yet so much has stayed the same. It's strange."

"It's good that you're back." Jake met her eyes again, this time with a bit more warmth in his smile. "I just wish you had arrived at a better time."

"Me, too." Maddie nodded. "I certainly didn't expect to come back home to this."

"I heard what you said." Jake's voice softened some as he looked over at her. "To Chuck."

"I was just apologizing for not being here. I left so

many friends behind." Maddie frowned as she wondered how much he might have heard. Had he been standing there watching the whole time?

"I understand that you want to do what you can to help, Maddie. But you really need to leave the investigation to me, and to my officers. It's important that the right steps are followed on this. Alright? None, of that sleuthing you did back in school." Jake turned and started to walk away.

"Sleuthing?" Maddie followed after him. "What do you mean?"

"Oh, don't think I've forgotten about that big scandal you caused by investigating the principal in middle school." Jake quirked an eyebrow as he stepped onto the path that led to the parking lot. "You've got that curious spirit in you, you've always had it. You've always wanted to get to the truth."

"Wow!" Maddie laughed as her mind flooded with memories. "I'd forgotten all about that. I almost got myself arrested, didn't I?"

Jake stared straight at her as he placed his hat back on the top of his head. "Yes, you did. I'd rather avoid a repeat of that. Alright?"

"I'd never let you cuff me, copper." Maddie grinned as she stepped past him in the direction of her car.

"Maddie, I'm serious." Jake began to follow after her. "A lot of things may have changed in Bayview, but the laws are the same."

"Don't worry, Jake." Maddie glanced back over her shoulder at him. "I'd never give you the pleasure."

"It wouldn't be a pleasure." Jake crossed his arms as she opened her car door.

"Well, lucky for us, we won't have to find out." Maddie settled in the driver's seat and pulled the door shut. As she started the engine, she caught him, still staring. She doubted that he was telling the truth. If she got into trouble when she was young, he'd always wanted her to be caught. She guessed that was one of the things about Bayview that hadn't changed at all.

As Maddie pulled away, he walked toward his patrol car. She looked in the rearview mirror as he jerked the door open, then slammed it shut. Yes, there was no doubt in her mind that Chief Jake Holden remembered her well.

CHAPTER 10

*A*s Maddie drove back toward her house, her thoughts lingered on Jake. She had a hard time seeing him as someone in authority when her mind traveled back to the comic books she'd seen on his bed, and the posters that hung up on his walls. Did he really grow up to be a superhero with a badge? She laughed at the thought. She guessed that the sleepy town of Bayview didn't require a lot of heroics. But then, that had changed yesterday, hadn't it?

No longer could she think of Bayview as a town where nothing ever happens. Something had happened. Something big. Maddie thought about his warning to stay out of the investigation. She didn't intend to do anything to interfere with it, but she did intend to keep her promise to Chuck. She just wasn't sure how. As she drove past town hall, she noticed a group of protesters clustered around the front steps. Each carried a sign with a different variation of the same theme: *Say No to Bayview Resort.*

Maddie pulled off to the side of the road, curious about what had prompted their protest. From what she remembered, there wasn't usually much dissension in the small town. As she approached the group, their chants grew louder.

"We don't need their money! We don't need their money!"

"What's this all about?" Maddie paused beside one of the women who held up a sign.

"You haven't heard?" She frowned. "Are you new in town?"

"Yes, I just moved back. Is this about the resort that everyone wants built?" Maddie raised an eyebrow.

"Not everyone." She lowered her sign. "We don't want it. We don't want it destroying our natural spaces and threatening the species that call our woodlands home."

"The amusement park would be a much better option. It will bring in extra business." A man beside her spoke up. "It's going to be far more contained and built on the property of an abandoned factory. It's not going to threaten any natural areas."

"Or any homes." An older man stepped forward, his voice stern as he spoke. "If they build this resort, they are going to bulldoze my home! I've lived in it all my life! What right do they have to take that away from me?"

"I'm so sorry to hear that." Maddie frowned as she studied the man. Something about him was familiar to her, but she couldn't quite place it. "Are they offering you a fair sum for it?"

"It's not about the money!" His voice raised to nearly a shout. "I don't want their money! I want my home! It's not for sale!" He thrust his sign up into the air above his head. "We don't need their money! We don't need their money!"

"Of course, I can understand that." Maddie recalled how hard it was for her to sell the home she'd raised her children in. "I recently had to sell my home, and it broke my heart." She sighed as she took a step back from him. "But I had no choice."

"I do." He looked into her eyes. "I can fight. That's what I choose to do. They can try to take my house, but they're not going to win!"

"It's not a done deal, yet, right?" Maddie glanced around at the other protesters. "It hasn't gotten approval?"

"Not yet. It was a sure thing before, but now." The woman she'd first spoken to winced.

"Now that Helen is dead, we stand a chance." The man who stood close to her raised his sign again. "She was the driving force behind all of this. Now that she's gone, I might be able to save my house."

Maddie's muscles tensed at the tone in his voice.

Clearly he was furious at the thought of losing his home. But did he have to sound so relieved over Helen's murder? The idea left her uneasy.

"She must have had a good reason to want the resort to be built here. Right? Would it benefit the community?" Maddie looked over the faces around her. "Can anyone tell me the whole story?"

"The whole story is that she was friends with the owner of the corporation who wanted to build the resort. She promised him that she would be able to get approval, and she just about got it," the woman beside Maddie replied.

"We need to make sure it's not approved," another woman shouted.

"The resort would only benefit the wealthy. It would be all inclusive, which means the guests would go to the restaurants in the resort, not our restaurants. It would take over a large portion of our harbor and make it inaccessible to the local residents." The woman scowled.

"It would ruin our town." The man beside her growled.

"Helen claimed it would bump up our tax revenue but the truth is it would increase the property taxes of everyone here. We all know that these big corporations hire people to help them get out of paying a dime in taxes. There's no way Bayview would see any of that money." The woman shook her head as she leaned on her sign. "Helen painted a pretty picture, and then she leaned on everyone and intimidated those who refused to comply. She wasn't going to give up until she got what she wanted. But now, we have a chance to change that."

"Because of her death?" Maddie gazed at the woman. "Don't you think that's in bad taste?"

"I'm not glad she's dead. I wouldn't wish that on anyone." She shook her head. "But that doesn't mean I won't take advantage of the opportunity to try to save our community."

"I don't mind at all that she's dead." The older man thrust his sign into the air again. "We don't need their money!"

Maddie stared at him for a long moment. He definitely did look familiar. His sharp, brown eyes, and his thick, black hair reminded her of someone. She just couldn't remember who. He looked a few years older than her, and he was quite attractive, with a strong frame. She guessed that he would have the strength to hurt Helen, if he wanted to. A scenario played out in her mind, of the pair arguing by the water. Maybe he had lost his temper? Maybe he hadn't meant to kill her?

Maddie's throat grew dry as she watched his muscles flex with each thrust of the sign into the air. Yes, he could be an intimidating person. Had Helen been frightened? Or had she really believed that she was untouchable?

As Maddie walked away from the protesters, her

heart raced. Bayview had never exactly been peaceful. There was so much struggle after the highway was built. People were desperate. But they had come together as a town to support each other. This didn't feel like coming together. It felt like Bayview was being torn apart.

CHAPTER 11

On the rest of Maddie's drive back to her house, she thought about what she had learned. If someone had decided that Helen had to die, would they decide that other people did, too? If the person who had killed her, did so, as some misguided effort to protect the town, would other people pose that same threat? If that was the case, the murderer had to be caught, and quickly.

Greeted at the front door by Bella and Polly, she felt the comfort of their loyalty and love. She sat down on the floor with them and let them pile up in her lap. As they licked her cheeks and wiggled back and forth to try to get as close as possible, she began to relax. She still had the power to help catch the murderer. She couldn't just sit back and let the police handle it. Not when she had a sharp mind, and a determination to find out exactly what had happened to Helen.

After throwing the ball to Bella and Polly for a while, Maddie set up her computer on the kitchen table and began searching for information about the protesters. She wanted to organize one of the rooms as an office to work out of, but that could wait, the kitchen table would be fine for now. It didn't take long for her to come across video testimonials of many of the people she'd seen at town hall that day, including the man she considered a suspect.

"My name is Peter Wilcox, and I am not going to surrender." He stared hard into the camera as he continued to speak.

Maddie noticed how serious he looked.

"I have lived in my home for my entire life. My mother passed it down to me when she died, when I was only twenty-five. Since then, I have taken care of every part of it, from the paint to every single nail in the roof. I have made sure that every plant has had nourishment, and that the windows stay clean. It's not just a house, it's my home, and I have invested all of myself into it." Peter took a breath, then sighed.

Maddie thought maybe he had finished his rant, but he kept going.

"To say to me that you have the right to bulldoze down my house, even though I own it outright, and I have never caused any problems, is just a terrible thing. It's downright wrong. I can't imagine anyone allowing this, and yet, Bayview is considering it."

Peter narrowed his eyes and leaned closer to the camera.

Maddie leaned forward, eager to know what he was going to say.

"I will tell you right now, if you try to bulldoze down my house, you will have to bulldoze me inside of it. Do you want your luxury resort enough to commit murder, Helen?" Peter pointed his finger at the camera. "You know as well as I do that the amusement park the Billings boys want to build would be just fine. But it's not good enough for you. You want more. You're willing to destroy some of our natural resources, as well as my house, and my life. All so you can have the luxurious lifestyle you're used to." He shook his head. "You're not even from Bayview. If it were up to me, you wouldn't have a single say in what is happening here."

Peter leaned forward and the video shut off.

"Wow." Maddie sat back as she stared at the screen. "Definitely plenty of hate in those words." As she played the video again, she noticed the sense of familiarity she felt with him. It wasn't his features, but the sound of his voice, and the steady gaze of his eyes. She didn't recognize the name, but she was certain that she had seen him somewhere before. She guessed that he had been around when she was growing up, but she simply couldn't place him.

His comments about the Billings boys caught Maddie's attention on the second play. Who were they? She did a quick search of the name on a social media page for the town. Many results came up. She noticed a few posted by a Benjamin Billings, and Bob Billings. She clicked on Benjamin's posts and discovered they centered around a small amusement park that the brothers wanted to build. He described it as a great resource for the town's youth, not only as a place for them to play, but also for potential job opportunities.

His brother later posted a similar topic and pointed out that the amusement park which would be built at the end of the harbor would be contained to a much smaller area than the luxury resort that would take up most of the area near the harbor. So, Bayview would get extra business but the natural land wouldn't be destroyed and overrun by too many tourists. Both brothers insisted they would limit their food options and encourage those that attended the park to patronize local restaurants.

Many people responded with support, but a few others reacted in opposition. She noticed right away that Helen was one of them. Her comments were sharp and numerous. She accused the brothers of having no business sense and bringing a disaster to the town. She pointed out how noisy it would be, and the amount of traffic it would create on a daily basis. The brothers fired back with plans for noise reduction and how they would encourage the tourists to stay in the town to bring more revenue to the local businesses.

As Maddie read over the online arguments, she saw that they escalated and became more heated with every post. Neither Billings could make a post without Helen responding to it, and although it seemed that things always started out civil, the comments evolved into chaos. There appeared to be an even divide of people who supported the amusement park and people who supported the luxury resort.

Maddie closed her computer and wiped at her eyes. Although she'd tried to keep up with the times when it came to technology, social media was not one of her favorite things. She found the tendency to be cruel and sarcastic to be a bit too much for her to take. It always stunned her, the things that people would say from behind a screen, compared to what they would be willing to say in person. Still, the resource had given her a good amount of information about the Billings and their plans. It had also made it clear that they and Helen were in quite a conflict before she died. Could her refusal to consider their idea and her determination to steer the town away from their plan be enough motive for them to cause her harm?

Without having any personal knowledge of the brothers, she knew she needed to find out more about them. She didn't want to read about them on a screen, though. She wanted to get a real person's point of view.

Maddie pulled out her phone and sent a text to Amber inviting her to lunch. Amber was the one person she knew she could trust in the town, and whose opinion she held very high. After getting a response that she'd be happy to meet her, she made sure the dogs' water bowls were full and headed for the door.

"I won't be long." Maddie called out to the dogs.

As Maddie pulled the door closed behind her, she was already eager to get back to spend more time with them. She spent a lot of her time with them back home, but she didn't have nearly enough funds to support herself. In between getting settled she needed to find a job. She had some bookkeeping clients but that wasn't enough to pay the bills, she needed to find more work. Which meant leaving her precious girls at home most of the day. She could hire someone to check in on them if necessary, but she knew it wouldn't be the same.

Craig had been a private investigator and she had worked as his assistant. Their office was a cottage in the back garden, so she had always been able to check on them during the day. She missed helping on his investigations and the flexibility the job provided. She often thought that she was the one that wanted to solve the cases more than him. She'd always loved a good mystery.

CHAPTER 12

*M*addie pulled into the parking lot of Janet's Place and noticed Amber near the front door. For a moment her thoughts flashed back to a time when Amber would greet her at the door of her parents' bakery. She always had an appetite and would beat Maddie there any time they planned to meet. She smiled some at the memory.

As they settled at a table, Amber smiled at her.

"This brings back old times, always meeting up for lunch, doesn't it?"

"It sure does." Maddie nodded. "We had some great food and memories eating here and at the bakery."

"I've been meaning to ask you what you're planning on doing with that property," Amber paused as the waitress arrived. Once they had placed their orders, she looked back at Maddie. "Any thoughts?"

"I guess, I'll sell it." Maddie shrugged. "I have to see what kind of shape it's in and decide what to do from there. But Tammy owns part of it, so I'll have to check with her before I do anything." She waved her hand. "But that's not important right now. What can you tell me about Benjamin and Bob Billings?"

"The Billings boys?" Amber glanced around the restaurant, which only had a few diners, then looked back at her. "That's quite a powder keg, what do you want to know?"

Maddie detected tension in Amber's tight frown and folded hands.

"They're planning to build an amusement park?" Maddie frowned. "Is it that dangerous to talk about them?"

"No, I guess not, with Helen gone now. That's still hard for me to believe." Amber sighed, then lowered her voice. "Bob and Benjamin grew up here, but they had some trouble in their teens. Well, lots of trouble." She gave a short laugh. "Let's just say they had Jake running all around this town."

"Speaking of Jake, how in the world did he get to be police chief?" Maddie smacked her hand lightly on the table. "I didn't see that coming."

"Oh no! I bet you didn't even recognize him." Amber grinned. "He has aged quite well, hasn't he?"

"Yes, he certainly has!" Maddie rolled her eyes, then laughed. "I think he was shocked that I didn't remember him."

"Of course he was." Amber leaned forward. "He was so excited when I told him you were moving back to town."

"Excited?" Maddie raised her eyebrows. "He certainly didn't act like that."

"Well, this is probably the first murder he's handled." Amber thanked the waitress as she brought their food. "But trust me, he was thrilled."

Maddie thought of the way he'd looked at her, and spoken to her, none of that conveyed thrilled to her. Still, she decided not to question it. Amber had always been optimistic and positive.

"Enough about Jake. What about these brothers? Did they do anything too terrible?" Maddie stuck her fork in the salad she'd ordered, though she didn't have much desire for it.

"A felony or two. Then they each did a stint in rehab. Jake gave them a lot more chances than he probably should have. But he worked hard to get them cleaned up. They've both been doing pretty well for a year or two. When the news broke that the town was going to be revitalized and there was money up for grabs, they came up with this amusement park idea. Helen jumped right in with the luxury resort idea. Then they went to war. It had gotten pretty ugly." Amber winced. "But I guess all of that is over now."

"I'm not so sure about that. I saw a group of protesters outside town hall. They all looked pretty angry." Maddie took a bite of her salad and immediately regretted not ordering the burger and fries she really wanted. "Do you think the Billings might have had something to do with Helen's death? It's a good way to guarantee that their idea stood a better chance of succeeding."

"Wow." Amber wiped her mouth of the ketchup that dripped off her burger. "That's quite an accusation." She eyed Maddie's salad. "Do you want some of my fries?"

"Yes, please. You can just pile them on top of the lettuce." Maddie laughed as she nudged her bowl forward. "I've been trying to watch my diet."

"But you look fantastic." Amber gave her thigh a light pat. "Not like me, I've been packing on the pounds lately. Not that I'm surprised. I'm certainly not eating as healthily as I used to."

"Amber, you've always had a gorgeous figure, and you still do." Maddie grinned. "I'm just trying to be more careful now that I'm getting older. Now that Craig is practically out of the kids' lives, I don't want to put my kids through losing me."

"Oh, sweetie." Amber gave her hand a squeeze. "I hadn't even thought of that. I'm sorry. Not having kids, it didn't cross my mind. And after marriage number two didn't work out, I've pretty much given up on any long-term romance."

"I didn't know you married again." Maddie's eyes widened. "You never told me. I would have come to the wedding."

"Oh, there wasn't one. It was the shortest marriage ever. We didn't last six months. We decided we wanted to keep things light for the ceremony, and it's a good thing we did. By the time I was divorced, half of my friends hadn't even realized I'd gotten married in the first place." Amber laughed. "But we live and learn right?"

"I'm sorry." Maddie looked into Amber's eyes. "It must have been hard to go through that."

"It wasn't the best time in my life." Amber sighed, then shook her head. "But things are better now. Especially with you here."

"I feel the same way." Maddie smiled. "I'm so glad that we can share lunch together again."

"So, what's your next step in all of this? I know that look in your eyes, I know that you're going to get to the bottom of it all. You never could let a mystery go unsolved. How can I help?" Amber pushed a few more of her fries onto Maddie's salad.

"I think I'm going to speak to Helen's neighbors. I know that around here, your neighbors know everything about you. I thought I might speak to them about what they know about Helen. What do you think? Will they talk to me?" Maddie quickly picked up the fries.

"I think that it's worth a try. Actually, Nancy is Helen's neighbor. Her only one." Amber glanced around, then lowered her voice. "And, I'd say she knows a good bit about her."

"Wait a minute. Nancy? The woman I met yesterday?" Maddie's eyes widened. "I didn't realize she was Helen's neighbor."

"Yes, she is. I'm sure she'd talk to you about anything she knows. She kept an eye on her, let's just leave it at that." Amber finished the last bite of her burger.

"I'd rather you told me more about this." Maddie set some money down on the table to cover the meal. "Please?"

"Nancy is normally a very mild-mannered person. She has never said a cross word to anyone, aside from her husband, that I can recall. But she was quite upset about the idea of the resort being built. She is very fond of the wooded area that they intended to fell to build it." Amber shrugged. "She didn't say anything at first, because she was sure that Helen would find a way to ruin her life, if she spoke up. But the other night, she finally said something at the meeting. I think she finally got sick of keeping quiet, she wanted to stop Helen. She started going to the protests. She had been documenting Helen's interactions with others, she was trying to prove that Helen was up to no good."

"Did she get proof?" Maddie scooted her chair forward and looked into Amber's eyes.

"I don't think so." Amber shook her head. "If she did, she never told me."

"Interesting." Maddie tapped her fingertips on the

table. "I think it's time I find out a bit more about all of this. Thanks for having lunch with me, Amber."

They stood up and headed toward the door.

"Let me know, if you need my help with anything." Amber followed her outside.

"Thanks, I will." Maddie hugged her, then hurried to her car. There was one person she could count on telling her the full truth about Helen. He was so angry, that she doubted he would hold anything back. If she could get some more information from him, she might be able to confirm it when she spoke to Nancy.

CHAPTER 13

*A*s Maddie drove away from the restaurant, she thought about what it might be like for Peter to be faced with the loss of his beloved home. She had an understanding of how it would feel, since she'd been forced to give up her own home. The shock she felt as the lawyer explained to her that not only did she not own her home, but that a second mortgage had been taken out on it, was something she would not soon forget.

Maddie's thoughts began to swirl as she once again tried to work out how Craig had kept so many secrets from her. How could he lie to her for so long? She had blamed herself at first. Maybe she was a bad wife? Maybe she should have realized what was happening? Everyone around her told her that there was no way that she could have known. It wasn't her fault.

Maddie was beginning to realize that they were

right. Only Craig was to blame for what had happened. He was so deceitful. He had hidden years of infidelity, gambling and bad investments from her. The extent of his deceit was only revealed when he had been arrested for fraud and left her with no house and a mountain of debt. She had no idea he had been forging signatures on stolen checks. He had even forged her signature to borrow money.

By the time Maddie reached Peter's house, her mind was swimming with all the memories of Craig's deception. Yes, losing the house had been hard, losing her marriage had been so much harder. Finding out everything was a lie was even harder.

"This is a fresh start, Maddie." As she muttered the words, she realized that she was actually starting to believe them.

Now that the shock of what Craig had done was starting to dissipate, when she thought about the years she had spent with him, she was beginning to realize that although there were many amazing and happy moments, especially with her children, she had never really felt happy with her marriage, with her life. Everything centered around Craig's wishes and dreams and she was just plodding along doing what she could to make him happy. Maybe this really was the opportunity for her to start living her life to make herself happy.

Maddie stepped out of the car and walked slowly toward the front door, distracted by the tiny details in the landscaping that surrounded her. Everything from painted rocks to tiny castles hidden in bushes, and even a miniature, wooden bridge that crossed a small, man-made pond. She could see how much love had been poured into the home, little touches that wouldn't be able to be moved to a new place. As she neared the front door, she wondered if he would even be willing to speak to her. She thought up a ruse just as she raised her hand to knock. Before she could, the door swung open.

"Yes?" Peter stared out at her, a hint of a smile on his lips.

"Sorry to disturb you. I'm a reporter, and I'd like some more information about your plight." Maddie gestured to the house in front of her. "And the possible loss of your home."

"A reporter, huh?" Peter grinned, then shook his head. "Maddie, I recognized you the moment I saw you. I just didn't think you recognized me. I guess I was right, and you didn't."

"I'm sorry?" Maddie stared into his eyes. "I thought I recognized you, too, but I wasn't sure from where."

"It's alright. I didn't always go by Peter. People knew me by my middle name, Ross." He brushed a few strands of his hair back from his eyes.

"Ross?" Maddie's heartbeat quickened at the mention of his name. Yes, she definitely remembered Ross.

"Good to see you again, Maddie." Peter chuckled, then pushed the door open wider. "Come inside, before someone drives by and throws a tomato at you for talking to me."

"Oh, I'm sure it's not that bad." Maddie stepped inside, still flustered by the revelation. "Wow, I can't believe that I didn't recognize you."

"I can. It's only been about thirty years." Peter looked over his shoulder at her as he led her into the living room. "But you remember me now?"

"Yes, of course. You used to work for my parents. They were always so grateful for your help." Maddie settled on one side of the couch and he settled on the other side.

"Maddie, I swear, you are just as pretty now as you always were." Peter shook his head as he smiled at her.

"Stop!" Maddie laughed. "You're just being kind."

"I'm serious." Peter sighed as he sat back against the couch. "Of course, I didn't see you that way then. You were just the kid that helped me knead the bread."

Maddie bit into her bottom lip as she fought the desire to confess that she had definitely looked at him that way then. She'd had the biggest crush on eighteen-year-old Ross who made the most delicious bread. But she had been a thirteen-year-old girl with no hope of getting his attention.

"I'm surprised you're still here after all these years.

I thought you might have moved on to greener pastures."

"I love it here." Peter shrugged. "At least I did. Until Helen showed up." He wiped his hand across his face. "I never thought I'd see a day when my home would be taken from me."

"Me, either," Maddie murmured, then forced a smile when he looked over at her. "Never mind that, it's a long story. I'm here because I want to know more about yours."

"I'm guessing you're not actually a reporter?" Peter laughed.

"No, I'm not. I'll confess. I'm the one that found Helen in the bay, and ever since, I've been determined to find out what happened to her. I thought you might be able to tell me more about it." Maddie looked into his eyes. "Since you seemed to be at odds with her."

"At odds is putting it very politely." Peter gritted his teeth. "That woman, she just couldn't hear reason. Or didn't want to. You would think with her being married to Chuck, she would have had some sense of loyalty to Bayview, but she didn't, and it got even worse after Chuck died."

"I'm sorry to hear that." Maddie folded her hands in her lap as she looked over the decor in the living room. It was simple, and clean. Everything had its place. "And I'm sorry that you're going through all of this. I don't see how they could justify taking your home."

"It's all a bunch of legal nonsense to me." Peter frowned. "I do have a lawyer working on it, but I'm not a wealthy man. I'm just a carpenter who likes baking." He paused, then looked over at her. "It looks like the house has stood up well."

"Nothing that a good clean and a coat of paint won't fix." Maddie rubbed her hands across her knees. "Once I find some more work, I'll be able to get it all sorted out."

"I'd be happy to help you." Peter smiled. "But I think we need to make something very clear between us, don't you?"

Maddie held her breath as she wondered if he knew about that crush she'd had on him so long ago. As she nodded, he smiled again.

"When you were a kid, if there was a mystery, you always wanted to solve it. I know you came here to find out more information about Helen's death. My guess is you came here to find out if I had a hand in it." Peter spread out his hands in front of him, revealing the well-worn skin of his palms, marked with small scars and callouses. "Maddie, I promise you, I had nothing to do with Helen's murder."

"I wasn't thinking that." Maddie's cheeks warmed as she glanced down at her hands.

"I just wanted you to be sure." Peter nodded. "So, did you move here with your husband?"

"No," Maddie tried to keep her voice even. "I'm divorced. Is there anyone in your life?"

"I'm seeing someone." Peter's eyes lit up. "But it's early days."

"That's exciting." Maddie smiled. Now, that she was long over her teenage crush, she hoped they could be friends. As long as he wasn't a murderer, that is.

"It is." Peter stood up. "I hope I've answered all of your questions, but if you have any more, I'll be over tomorrow to drop off some paint. I have some left over from when I painted this place." He gestured to his house. "I'm sure you could use it."

Maddie stood up as well. "Really Peter, you don't have to do that."

"I want to." Peter walked her to the door. "As long as you don't mind me popping over, that is."

"Not at all." Maddie smiled as she stepped through the door. "It was good to see you again."

"I think we'll be seeing a lot more of each other." Peter glanced past her, out the door, at the long road that led to his house. "At least, until the bulldozer shows up."

"Try not to worry too much, Peter, we're going to get this all figured out. Now that Helen is dead, I hear the resort probably won't be built." As her own words hung in the air between them, Maddie wondered if it would all work out okay. She was determined to do everything she could to make sure it did. It seemed to her that just about everything was out of her hands lately. But she intended to change that. She was going to take control.

CHAPTER 14

*I*t was easy for Maddie to navigate her way to Helen's house. Everyone in town knew where she lived. Despite the home being well-kept, it stood out from the other properties nearby. Its paint was bright, its fixtures modern, and the landscaping looked as if it belonged on the grounds of a castle, not a simple house. It was clear to her that Helen definitely had higher aspirations of what her life was supposed to be like.

Maddie parked along the road between Helen's house and the house beside it. Although there wasn't any police tape surrounding the house, there was a note posted on the front door, that she guessed declared the home under investigation by the police. As tempted as she was to try to get inside, she could only imagine Jake's reaction to that. She had assured him he wouldn't have the chance to put her in handcuffs, and she hoped to keep that promise.

As Maddie stepped out of the car, she noticed a woman in the front window of the neighboring house. It took her only a second to recognize her as Nancy, the woman she'd met the day before. She stared at Maddie for a long moment, then walked away from the window. By the time she made it to the front door of the bungalow, Nancy had opened it.

"Can I help you?" Nancy peered out at her with a hint of apprehension in her voice.

"Hi Nancy. I'm Maddie, we met yesterday. Do you remember?" Maddie smiled.

"Yes, of course." Nancy looked past her, at the street, then back into her eyes. "What are you doing here?"

"Sorry to intrude, I just thought maybe I could ask you a few questions about Helen, since you were her neighbor." Maddie caught movement in the house beyond Nancy, out of the corner of her eye. A moment later, a man walked back through the living room and paused behind Nancy.

"Who is it, Nance?"

"Her name is Maddie." Nancy looked over her shoulder at the man who stood quite a bit taller than her. "She's a friend of Amber's."

"Oh." He nodded to Maddie as he continued to hover behind Nancy. "Don't make her stand outside, bring her in."

"I'm not sure that's a good idea." Nancy frowned, even as she stepped back from the door. "Maddie, this is my husband, Max." She gestured to the man who held out his hand to Maddie.

"Nice to meet you, Max." Maddie gave his hand a quick shake. "I hope I didn't interrupt anything. I actually grew up around here, and I've just recently moved back. I'm trying to get to know the area again."

"Maddie." Max nodded as his hand fell back to his side. "I heard that you were the one who found Helen's body. Is that true?"

"Yes, unfortunately I did." Maddie noticed that Max wasn't just tall, he was very muscular as well.

"I'm so sorry, that must have been terrible." Nancy closed the door behind her. "Sorry for being so hesitant, but we've had a parade of visitors today, and you are the first friendly face."

"Oh?" Maddie frowned. "I'm sorry to hear that. No one too troublesome, I hope?"

"Just Chief Holden." Max quickly gathered together some papers on the coffee table and piled them onto an empty, wooden chair near the dining room.

Maddie caught sight of them as he moved them. They were fliers supporting the protests. She looked up at Max.

"Why was he here?"

"He's interviewing everyone he thinks might have

had issues with Helen." Max shrugged. "I told Nancy not to worry about it, but she is terribly offended."

"And why shouldn't I be?" Nancy snapped her words. "That man came into our home and accused us of such horrible things!"

"He didn't accuse us, Nancy. You're exaggerating." Max huffed as he sat down hard in an overstuffed recliner. "You and I both know that after that meeting at town hall, you got into an argument with Helen. You can't just expect him to ignore that."

"So what? Everyone argued with Helen! I wasn't the only one. I'm not any more suspicious than anyone else." Nancy crossed her arms as she sat down on one side of the couch and gestured for Maddie to sit on the other.

"I think we all want to figure out what happened." Maddie sat down as she offered a small smile. "I'm guessing Chief Holden is under a lot of pressure to find the truth. I'm sure he's just being thorough."

"There's no need to be thorough with me." Nancy crossed her arms. "I've never committed anything close to a crime in my entire life. He's targeting us because we have been at the protests, and he doesn't like them. He thinks we all need to just be quiet about everything and let things happen."

"He supports the luxury resort?" Maddie's eyes widened at the thought.

"He doesn't say." Max huffed as he looked over at

his wife. "But according to Nancy, his silence on the subject speaks volumes."

"Well, it does, doesn't it?" Nancy shook her head. "If he wanted to protect Bayview, he would take a stand. Instead, he hovers over the protesters like we're all a bunch of criminals ganging together to cause havoc."

"I see." Maddie narrowed her eyes. "Did you ever see him spending time with Helen? Showing a special interest in her?"

"No, there was nothing like that." Max frowned. "Listen, I think you need to understand something. This town was divided by all of this. People had to choose sides. Chief Holden didn't. I admire him for that. He needs to stay neutral as the law enforcement in this town."

"Such rubbish. He should voice his opinion." Nancy rolled her eyes. "Look, we all know that Helen didn't want what was best for this town, she just wanted what was best for herself."

"Did you know her well?" Maddie asked.

"Well enough not to want to get to know her better. When Chuck was still alive, we would all have lunch sometimes. But once he died, the real Helen came out. She began stomping through this town like it was nothing to her. I can't tolerate someone who has no empathy for others." Nancy curled her upper lip and shook her head.

"See, that's the problem right there." Max growled

at her. "When you talk like that, you sound suspicious. If you really want Chief Holden to leave us alone, maybe you need to stop speaking up so much!"

"You're right." Nancy gritted her teeth as she stood up. Her tense shoulders and narrowed gaze gave away her anger, despite her words. "I'm sorry. I think you'll have to leave now, we have some things to do." She glanced over at Max.

"Of course." Maddie got to her feet. She managed one more quick look at the pile of papers before she let herself out.

As Maddie hurried to her car, she heard the first of what she was sure would be many shouts coming from the house. From the snippets she could hear, Nancy was clearly furious. It occurred to her that Helen might not have been the problematic neighbor. If Nancy and Max fought often, and loudly, she guessed that Helen didn't enjoy having to put up with it. It was clear that Nancy had a temper, but was that enough to consider her a killer?

CHAPTER 15

When Maddie pulled up outside her house, her phone beeped with a text. It was from her sister, Tammy.

Is it okay if I come to stay for a few days next week?

Maddie smiled at the thought and replied that she couldn't wait. When Maddie had told her sister that she planned to move back to Bayview, she immediately asked if she could visit. Her heart raced with excitement at the thought of seeing her.

As Maddie walked toward her house, she noticed a set of rocking chairs, a table, and chairs, where her empty porch used to be.

"What's this?" She laughed as she walked up the steps, then froze when her front door swung open.

"Maddie!" Amber smiled at her. "Sorry to barge in like this, but Mom decided we just had to come over for tea. She couldn't wait to see you."

"Oh, it's alright." Maddie grinned as she saw Amber's mother step out behind her.

"I hope you don't mind, your mother always made sure I had a key to the house. I wanted to surprise you." Iris smiled as she set a tray with teacups and saucers, down on the table. "I figured, we'll be doing a lot of visiting, so we'll need to be comfortable."

"This is amazing." Maddie took a deep breath as she enveloped Iris in a tight hug. She stepped back and gazed at her. From her white hair piled on the top of her head, to the long, flower-covered dress she wore, she couldn't have looked more different than her own mother did, and yet her entire presence reminded Maddie of the woman she'd lost. Her mother always insisted on making tea whenever someone stopped by. She would press them to stay, even if they only had a minute. "Thank you, so much, both of you." She settled into one of the chairs as Bella and Polly pranced out onto the porch. "I guess you met the girls, Iris?"

"Beautiful girls they are, and so well-mannered." Iris grinned as she reached down to pet them.

Maddie smiled to herself as she knew how mischievous they could be.

"I just spoke with Nancy." She took a cup of tea from Iris. "This is a nice change after that."

"Oh, let me guess, Max was home?" Amber gave a short laugh. "Those two are like oil and water."

"And yet, they have stuck together for quite some

time." Iris shook her head. "I don't see how they've managed to stay together. But all relationships are different, I guess."

"What were they fighting about this time?" Amber met her eyes.

"Actually, over whether Nancy was acting suspicious. He thought she was talking too much about her feelings for Helen. I guess, the police have found out about her recent comments against both the resort and Helen and are questioning her about them." Maddie frowned. "I really don't know what to think. She certainly seems to have a temper. At least toward her husband."

"That's true, she does." Amber swirled her tea in her cup as she looked down into it. "But she doesn't have any history of violence that I've heard about."

"Helen wasn't exactly squeaky clean herself." Iris took a sip of her tea, then looked at Maddie over the rim of the cup.

"No?" Maddie smiled as she knew that Iris wanted her to be intrigued. "Is there something that I should know?"

"Hm, should you?" Iris set the cup down on the saucer in front of her and glanced over at her daughter. "I don't like to speak out of turn."

"Sure, Mom." Amber laughed as she met her mother's eyes. "Maddie knows you just about as well as I do, so don't try to pull the wool over her eyes."

"Okay, okay." Iris sighed, then lowered her voice. "Helen was not faithful to Chuck."

"Really?" Maddie's eyes widened at the thought. "Everyone I spoke to indicated that their marriage was strong."

"It was quite some time ago, ten years or even more, I believe." Iris added a cube of sugar to her tea. "She took up with a man in town. A much older, married man."

"Wow." Maddie clucked her tongue. "It surprises me that she could get away with that around here."

"She didn't. At least, not for long. The story goes that she had this man wrapped around her finger, and he decided that he was going to divorce his wife, so that he could be with her. But Helen didn't have any interest in that and ended things after he left his wife." Iris stirred her tea and blew a snow white curl off her forehead. "Just like that, a family blown to bits."

"But this happened so long ago. I don't understand. Chuck and Helen were still married, weren't they?" Maddie looked between the two women.

"Yes, they were." Amber nodded. "They never split up."

"They almost did." Iris took another sip of her tea. "Chuck lived with his mother for I'd say a good two weeks before he decided to go back to Helen. I think he just loved her so much, he couldn't let her go, even after the way she treated him."

"Poor Chuck." Maddie felt a sting as her husband's betrayal surfaced. "He must have been heartbroken."

"If he was, he didn't show it. Within a month or so they were all around town together, as if nothing had ever happened. Unfortunately, the man she had an affair with didn't fare so well. His wife was not forgiving, and his daughter probably suffered the most." Iris sighed as she shook her head. "I know, I know, things are different these days. But when I think of all of the chaos it caused, for two people to be so selfish, it just irks me."

"People make mistakes, Mom." Amber shrugged, then sighed. "I sure made plenty."

"But you never cheated on anyone. You never hurt anyone that way." Iris set her cup down hard. "That's just terrible."

"There are many ways to break someone's heart." Amber took a sip of tea.

"Yes, yes, there are." Maddie nodded. "My husband was wonderful in so many ways, but the secrets he kept broke my heart."

"I'm so sorry, Maddie." Amber frowned as she placed her hand on top of Maddie's. "I know how that feels. I've basically given up on a serious relationship. We're too old for all of that now, aren't we?"

"No." Maddie squeezed her hand. "No, I don't think we are, Amber. I am coming to realize that as hurt as I am by everything that Craig hid from me, from how he betrayed me, I wouldn't trade the time we shared. It was worth it. I have three beautiful kids because of him. I think, even though it may be a struggle, it's still worth it to try to keep your heart open. I believe your time is still coming."

"Maybe." Amber tipped her head from side to side. "I guess we'll just have to wait and see."

"Just wait until you girls get to be my age." Iris laughed. "Then you'll just be glad that everyone is finally leaving you alone!"

"You'll never be alone, Mom." Amber leaned over and hugged her mother. "I promise."

"You make me the luckiest mother around." Iris grinned as she hugged her back. "I have to say, looking back on life, I do treasure the memories of the times I shared with the loves of my life, and I do mean more than one. I feel as if now that I'm getting older, I'm starting to truly reflect on the value of life." She waved her hand, then sighed. "But we're not here to discuss all of that, are we? What we need to figure out is, who killed Helen?"

"Oh, I don't want you to get involved in all of that." Maddie shook her head. "It's a little mission of mine, but it could certainly turn out to be dangerous."

"Do you hear this child?" Iris burst into laughter as she looked at Amber. "She thinks she's going to scare me off with a little danger?"

"Ah, yes." Amber winced. "Maddie, in case you've forgotten, my mother does whatever she puts her mind to, no matter what anyone says. In fact, I think you two share that quality."

"I suppose we do." Maddie grinned. "Your help is welcomed, Iris. Please forgive me for forgetting just how determined you can be."

"I'll forgive you, but just this once." Iris held up one finger. "No second chances with me." She took a breath, then looked out over the water. "It's hard to believe that Helen drew her last breath not far from here. She may not have been my favorite person, but she was still a member of this community, and we must get to the truth."

As Maddie finished her tea, she felt warmth spread through her, not just from the hot liquid, or the kind gifts from Amber and Iris, but from the sense of community that she had always felt in Bayview.

Maddie walked Amber and Iris down the driveway as they headed back to their car. Once they reached it, Iris turned to face Maddie.

"I probably shouldn't tell you this, because I don't think she was involved. But the married man that Helen had an affair with was Frances' father." Iris locked her eyes to Maddie's. "Please don't take that to mean that I think Frances had anything to do with this. But I'm sure it's going to come up in the investigation."

"Frances' father?" Maddie took a sharp breath. "How terrible for her. And her poor mother."

"Vera didn't take it well at all. She's only still quite

young, but she lives in St. Frederick's, the retirement community, now. She's become very reclusive. Stays in her room most of the time, keeps to herself mainly." Iris shook her head. "I try and help her, but she just turns me away."

"That's terrible. How sad." Maddie frowned.

"Yes." Iris clucked her tongue. "Frances has been through a lot, but she's not a murderer. I just don't believe it could be true."

Iris settled in the car.

"Thanks for the information." Maddie wrapped her arms around Amber and squeezed. "And thank you for everything else, too."

"Good luck." Amber walked around to the driver's side of the car.

Maddie's eyes settled on the car as it pulled out into the street. Iris' revelation left her heart pounding. Could Frances have been involved? She needed to know for sure. Was that why the officer had questioned her so intently? Before she could speak to Frances about it again, she wanted to find out more about her past. That meant a trip to St. Frederick's.

CHAPTER 16

*A*s Maddie drove toward St. Frederick's, she wondered if Vera would even see her, and if she did, how would she ask her the questions she wanted answered. She needed to tread carefully in order to help find out if Frances was possibly the murderer and make sure not to upset Vera.

After a brief discussion with the receptionist at the front desk, she was led into a visiting area. She noted the brightly colored paintings, the assortment of art supplies, and the wide open space that surrounded the cushioned chairs and small tables. She felt more relaxed just by being in the atmosphere. She settled into one of the soft chairs and felt as if it might swallow her up.

A woman about fifteen years her senior walked toward her. Her silver and black hair was smoothed back into a tight bun. Her slender frame barely filled out the blouse and trousers she wore.

"Vera, how are you today?" Maddie met her dark brown eyes.

"Everyone asks me that." Vera grinned as she settled in the chair across from her. "I just say, about the same." She shrugged. "Not much changes in my world."

"I really appreciate you taking the time to see me. I know you don't know me, but I'm a friend of your daughter's. Frances." Maddie smiled.

"Oh, my Fran." Vera closed her eyes as she nodded. "She's such a wonderful girl. I'm so lucky to have her."

"I was in her shop the other day and she made me the most beautiful bouquet. She has a real talent for it." Maddie braced herself as she wondered how Vera would react when she broached the sensitive topic of Helen's relationship with her husband.

"Yes, she has always had an ability to see and create beauty. But that's not why you're here." Vera crossed her arms as she sat back in her chair. Her smile faded, her eyes locked to Maddie's. "Please, don't waste your time on pretending. I can see right through all of that. People have been lying to me my entire life."

"I'm sorry." Maddie sensed that the woman had very little tolerance. One wrong word, and she wouldn't get an ounce of information from her. If she wanted honesty, then she had to go for it. "You're right. I'm not here because of your daughter. I'm here because of another woman."

"Helen." Vera supplied the name as she sighed. "Right?"

"You've heard?" Maddie stared back at her.

"About her death?" Vera nodded, then gestured to the large room around them. "I may keep to myself, but I'm not completely cut off from the rest of the world. We all hear about what happens on the outside. It usually makes us want to stay here all the more."

"It's quite shocking." Maddie rubbed her hands across her knees and sat forward. "Such a tragedy."

"A tragedy?" Vera laughed, then shook her head. "No, that woman's death is not a tragedy. The havoc she was causing is the tragedy. What she did to me, and my family, that's the tragedy."

"I've heard some things about that." Maddie did her best to hide her reaction to her words. Even if she held a grudge against the woman, how could she revel in her death?

"Oh, you have?" Vera sneered as she looked away from Maddie. "I guess you're an expert then."

"I didn't mean to imply that." Maddie shifted in her chair as her heart began to race. She sensed she was going to lose control of the conversation. "Vera, I didn't come here to cause any harm. I just wanted to see if you could give me any insight into what might have happened to Helen."

"There is no more harm that can be done to me." Vera pulled her feet up onto the chair and hugged her knees. "That happened long ago. Sometimes, things just can't be fixed."

"Do you mean your marriage?" Maddie frowned.

"It was more than that. That's what people don't understand. These days, everyone gets divorced, it's no big deal. But back then, it was different. It wasn't just my marriage that was destroyed, it was my family." Vera sighed.

"I'm so sorry." Maddie frowned.

"The pain I watched my daughter go through, and then we lost our home. I was so upset that I couldn't work, not that I made enough money to support us, anyway. Things got worse and worse. I tried to hold it together for Frances, but I just couldn't. I waited so long to have her, she was a miracle, and then I was so upset by everything, I couldn't even be a mother to her. Luckily, my sister took her in. She refused to live with her father. It was all just such a mess." Vera threw her hands in the air, then she met Maddie's eyes. "You probably think I'm cruel for saying this, but at least now, maybe, I can start to feel some peace. Helen's gone. Whatever happened, I can guarantee you she earned it. If that makes me a bad person, then so be it. But when someone's lies take everything from you, you'll understand." She stood up. "Now, I have to get going."

Maddie held her breath as she processed her

words. She certainly hadn't hidden her distaste for Helen. She obviously didn't want to discuss it anymore and she doubted she would get anything else out of her.

"Thank you for your time, Vera." Maddie stood up as well.

"That's okay." Vera smiled slightly. "I am glad that Helen is dead. If they ever find the murderer, bring them here, so I can congratulate them."

Maddie's mouth fell open at her words. She had no idea how to respond to her. She certainly had made her distaste for Helen obvious.

Maddie walked toward the door. She could empathize with Vera. Maddie knew what it was like to be lied to, to have those lies destroy what she held dear, and she knew it would have been much harder if her children were younger. She didn't think that Helen deserved to have been murdered, though.

Maddie thought through her encounter with Vera as she drove home. Even if she did have empathy for Vera, that didn't change the fact that she clearly had a strong motive to be involved in Helen's murder. So did her daughter. With Vera staying at the retirement village, had she pushed her daughter to take Helen's life? What about her ex-husband? He had left his marriage, and lost his daughter, all for Helen's love, only to find out that she didn't want anything to do with him. That would be enough to give someone motive as well. Tracking him down might be difficult, though, as from what she had heard, she guessed he didn't stick around Bayview to be ridiculed and judged by its residents. And would he hold a grudge for so long?

The moment Maddie walked in her door, her two dogs greeted her with happy barks and quick licks of her hands. She nuzzled into their furry cheeks.

"I think we all need some fresh air, huh?" Maddie opened the front door. "Let's go, come on out." She held the door open for Bella and Polly. They pranced across the front porch and down the steps to the front yard.

One thing Maddie liked about being back in Bayview was how quiet it was. There was barely a car on the road. She watched as the dogs ran around the fenced-in yard. Her parents loved dogs and always had at least one, so they had made sure that the property was safe for them. Bella and Polly could be cheeky, but they were very well-trained. Polly was definitely the more boisterous of the pair.

When Maddie noticed a car turn down the road and drive slowly toward her house, she called them back to her side. After a moment of confusion, she recognized the man who stepped out of the car. Peter. Yes, he was going to drop off some paint. She'd almost completely forgotten about it.

"Okay, we've got company. Be good!" Maddie smiled down at the dogs.

"I'll put these in the garage." Peter held up two paint cans.

"Thank you." Maddie walked over and opened the garage door for him.

"I'll leave these here." Peter placed the cans in the corner, then walked to his car. "I'll just be a second." He grabbed something from the back seat, then walked over to her.

"Thanks again for coming out, Peter." Maddie started up the porch steps.

"It's no problem, I'm happy to help." Peter followed her inside as the dogs clamored around him. "Cute pups."

"Yes, they're my loves. That's Bella, and that's Polly. They've been by my side for the past couple of years." Maddie reached down to pet both of them.

"I brought you some homemade bread." Peter handed her a loaf of bread. "It's sourdough."

"Oh, thank you, it smells delicious." Maddie smiled. "I'll just let the dogs out the back." She led him toward the kitchen.

"Are you staying?" Peter followed after her.

"I am, I haven't gotten around to unpacking yet." Maddie looked at the suitcases propped against the wall. "Although, there's not much to unpack, anyway."

"One of these days you're going to have to tell me the whole story about your journey back home." Peter looked out through the back window.

"One day." Maddie nodded. "How much do I owe you?"

"Nothing." Peter turned back to face her. "Your mother used to make me a fresh, home-cooked meal, if I brought the bread. I could sure use some good food and great company. What do you think? Tomorrow night? I can come over in the afternoon and we can have a look through the house to see if there's anything that needs fixing that I can help with, then we can have dinner?"

As Peter looked into her eyes, Maddie sensed that he was being more than kind. He genuinely wanted to spend time with her. It startled her to realize that.

"Yes." Maddie nodded as she smiled. "That sounds nice. It's been a while since I cooked for anyone. I have some recipes I'd love to try out."

"Great." Peter gave a short laugh. "I'm looking forward to it."

A sharp knock on the door drew Maddie's attention before she could reply.

"Expecting someone?" Peter raised an eyebrow.

"No, not at all." Maddie frowned. "I'll just see who it is."

The dogs raced past Maddie to the door. When she reached it to open it, the man on the other side peered through the window beside it at her.

"Jake?" Maddie took a slight step back as he pulled his hat off his head, then stepped closer to the door.

"Do you have a few minutes, Maddie?" Jake looked past her, at the man who stood only a few feet away. "Peter."

"Chief." Peter nodded to him. "I should be on my way, Maddie. I'll see you tomorrow."

Maddie watched as Jake's jaw tensed.

"Thank you for the bread." Maddie smiled as Peter stepped past her, then squeezed his way through the door, ensuring he kept a space between himself and Jake.

"No problem." Peter waved over his shoulder as he headed for his car.

Jake stared after him until the car started, then pulled away.

"Maddie, we need to talk." He crossed into the house, without being invited.

CHAPTER 17

"*J*ake, what's going on?" Maddie noticed the tension in his expression. "Did you find out something about Helen's murder?"

"Only that the man you just had in your house is one of the prime suspects. What are you thinking having him in your home? Alone?" Jake turned back to face her. "Did you know that he threatened Helen in the past?"

"I know that she was basically causing him to lose his home." Maddie watched him, wary of the authority in his tone. "I think anyone would be angry about that."

"Maybe so, but that doesn't mean that he has the right to threaten her." Jake ran his hand back through his hair as he sighed. "Why was he here?"

"That's really my business, isn't it? Why are you

here?" Maddie narrowed her eyes. "You still haven't told me."

"I'm here because I saw Peter's car out front on my way past and I wanted to make sure you were okay." Jake looked into her eyes.

"I'm fine." Maddie continued to keep a good amount of distance between them. "But you didn't have to come in here to check on me."

"I'm glad I did. Otherwise you might still be alone in this house with Peter." Jake shook his head. "You can't just let anyone into your home."

"Anyone?" Maddie laughed. "He's been a family friend for years. He worked at my parents' bakery."

"And that makes you feel safe with a murder suspect?" Jake pursed his lips.

"I've known him since I was young." Maddie shook her head as she avoided his frustrated gaze.

"You don't know him, now. You haven't known him for years. People change, Maddie." Jake stepped in front of her and managed to meet her eyes. "You can't take those kinds of risks."

"What do you care what kind of risks I take?" Maddie crossed her arms as Bella and Polly huddled close to her, on alert from the tension between her and Jake.

"Would you rather I didn't care?" Jake searched her eyes for a long moment, then looked away. "I don't want anyone else to be killed in Bayview. Is that so much to ask?"

"I'm not going to be killed." Maddie let her arms fall back to her sides as she noticed the sudden distance in his voice. "Your time and energy is better spent on finding the murderer than warning me about Peter."

"You can't be certain that it's not Peter." Jake glanced around the house. "I just want you to be careful. Things change a lot over the years."

"I knew him well enough then, and I know him well enough now." Maddie's heart pounded as she felt strange defending herself to a man who she didn't actually recognize as the boy she had once known. She felt that given Peter's history with her family, she needed to defend him, even though she didn't really know if he was guilty or not. "I hung on his every word when I was young, if there was an ounce of malice in him, I would have seen it!"

"Oh." Jake took a step back and sighed. "I see. This is a romantic situation." He narrowed his eyes. "That's even more dangerous. You can't let your feelings for him blind you to the possibility that he had something to do with this."

"I have no romantic feelings for him." Maddie shook her head. "Here you are focusing on Peter, when I just discovered that Helen had an affair with a married man. Have you even tracked him down to question him? Don't you think he might be more of a suspect than Peter? Maybe he wanted her back now and she rejected him? Or he blamed her for ruining his life? Who knows?"

"Of course, I've tracked him down. Why do you think I sent one of my officers to question Frances? Her father was one of the first people I tracked down. He has an airtight alibi. He wasn't even in the country at the time of Helen's murder." Jake's tone sharpened. "I think the problem here is that you don't think I'm capable of doing my job. You still see me as that skinny boy that you wanted nothing to do with in high school, don't you?"

"I'm not doubting your skills." Maddie frowned as she sensed a deeper hurt within him. "I don't know you, it's been years. All I know is that you seem to think a person I consider to be a good man is capable of murder, so who is doubting who here?"

"I'm just warning you that you have to look at him through open eyes, not through whatever leftover feelings for him you might be harboring." Jake sighed as he took a step back from her. "Just try to be clearheaded about it."

"I don't have feelings for him. Not anymore. Not that I really did then, either. I was just a kid." Maddie frowned as she tried to get a grasp on her thoughts. "Jake, you can't just come in here and tell me what to do. You say people change, but you certainly haven't. You're still trying to tell me what's best."

"Did you ever wonder why that was?" Jake's tone softened as he spoke.

"Why?" Maddie met his eyes as her heart skipped a beat.

"Never mind." Jake shook his head as he turned toward the door. "It's your life, Maddie, you're right." He paused at the door and looked back at her. "You can make your own decisions."

"Jake!"

Confusion rushed through her as he stepped through the door and closed it behind him. She was tempted to chase after him, but why? She felt tiny paws against her legs, and light licks on her fingertips. She began to relax as she crouched down to pet her dogs. They always had a way of comforting her no matter what situation she was in.

"I don't know, pups." Maddie sighed as she stared at the front door. "Maybe moving back to Bayview was a mistake."

Maddie heard the engine of Jake's patrol car fire up outside the door and closed her eyes. Had something happened in the past that affected his attitude toward her now? Had she slighted him in some way that he still held a grudge about? Her high school years weren't her proudest moments. She was caught up in teenage life, in boys, and dances, and friends.

Maddie could clearly remember more than one time when she'd been a bit harsh to Jake. But he was always there to warn her, to question her, to push for her to make a different choice. She never noticed him treating Amber the same way. If they were all at a party, Jake lingered by her side, even if she had a boyfriend on her arm. But why?

Maddie tried to recall what had happened when she had known him all those years ago. Things had changed between middle school, when he would tug at her hair, and high school, when she couldn't remember spending as much time with him. With so many years between then and now, it was almost impossible to sort through all of the memories. But she guessed that she'd done something during that time, something that he still carried, despite the decades they'd spent apart.

Maddie walked into the kitchen, followed by her dogs. She didn't doubt that she could have done something to hurt his feelings. But she would never have intentionally done so. But maybe she hadn't been as sensitive to them as she could have been. She had her first boyfriend during that time, had she just had less time for Jake? She fed the dogs, then began preparing a meal for herself.

Maddie could recall teaching all of her children to be kind to others, even those that they found to be annoying, or didn't fit in. She'd paid special attention to their friendships and encouraged them to not judge a book by its cover. But wasn't that what she'd done to Jake? She couldn't recall a specific time that she'd been cruel to him, but she knew that she'd tried to keep him on the outside of her circle. Was there something about him that had made her feel uneasy back then? If there was, she didn't feel the same way now. Instead, she felt a desire for his approval, or perhaps his forgiveness.

Then again, maybe his role of police chief had simply gone to his head. He'd always been protective of others. Maybe having the authority of a badge now made him think that others had to simply do whatever he said.

"I'm not sure, babies." Maddie finished the last bite of her chicken. "But we're going to have to figure all of this out, if we're going to stay here." She swept her gaze from the rafters to the floorboards. "And we don't have much other choice. So, we're going to have to make it work."

Polly gave a soft growl, then rolled over on her back for a belly rub.

Maddie rubbed her belly gently, then laughed as Bella flopped over, eager for the same treatment.

CHAPTER 18

*S*till unsettled by her encounter with Jake, Maddie set a teakettle on the stove and turned it on. As she waited for the water to heat up, she leaned her hands against the sink and looked out through the back window of the house. It overlooked a wide backyard surrounded by a natural fence, created by thick, towering trees. She had loved playing in that yard as a child. She imagined herself on adventures with fairies and dragons. Everything felt magical then. She smiled at the thought of her new granddaughter having some of those adventures as well.

Maddie gazed at one particular tree, her favorite, that she had spent hours in as a young teen, hiding from the pressures of teenage life. She'd curl up in the crook of its limbs and read her books for hours. She spent even more time dreaming about what her future would be like. Her thoughts were filled with all of the adventures she would have.

The shriek of the teakettle knocked her out of the trance she'd fallen into. She filled her cup with the hot liquid and dropped a tea bag into it.

Maddie breathed in the scent of the lemon and ginger, then headed for the front porch.

Bella and Polly trotted after her, eager to have some outside time. She sat down on the top step of the porch as the dogs tumbled around with each other in the yard. She took a sip of her tea, the tip of her tongue slightly singed by its heat and thought about living in Bayview. It was strange seeing people that she'd known a lifetime ago. In some ways Jake was right. They were strangers to her, even if she thought she knew them well. Even if being back in Bayview made it feel as if she had never left.

Maddie's cell phone rang in her pocket. The sharp sound jolted her, causing a few drops of tea to spill over the edge of the cup and land on the knee of her pants. She winced at the sudden heat, then fished her phone out of her pocket. The sight of her eldest daughter's name brought a smile to her lips.

"Sandy, how are you?"

"I'm okay, Mom, just tired."

"I bet." Maddie took another sip of her tea. "How are you feeling? Are you getting any rest at all?"

"Some. I'm doing okay, Mom, I promise." Sandy laughed. "You sound so worried."

"I'm sorry, honey. I know this can be a hard time. It's a wonderful time, but life with a baby can be exhausting. I just want to make sure you're being taken care of, because that's important, too."

"I know, you keep telling me." Sandy sighed.

"Something's wrong?" Maddie's senses sharpened at the hint of sadness in her voice.

"I just miss you, Mom."

"I miss you, too, sweetheart." Maddie's heart ached at the thought.

"I just wish we could live close to each other." Sandy's voice grew wistful. "I know it wasn't practical, but I wish you could have moved here instead of Bayview."

Although ever since Sandy moved away for college, she had lived a few hours drive away, Maddie had always wished they could live close by, especially now that she had Caitlyn. She had been to visit since Caitlyn had been born and she couldn't wait to see her granddaughter again.

"If you need me, I can be there in a second. I'll get a ticket right now." Maddie started to stand up.

"No, Mom. I'm okay, really. Scott is taking good care of both of us. I'm worried about you, though. After what happened with Dad, and then this sudden move. I just want to make sure that you're okay."

"Oh, Sandy." Maddie's eyes misted at the thought of her daughter, caught in the middle of new motherhood, still taking the time to worry about her mother. "You're such a caring person. I love you so much. But I am fine. I promise."

"I can't wait to visit. I'd love to see the house that you grew up in again. I can't remember it really. We haven't been there in so long. Maybe in a few weeks we can come? Maybe Laura can come as well?"

"Oh, that would be lovely. I can't wait to see all of you again." Maddie's voice raised slightly in anticipation. Her youngest daughter, Laura, was away at college. Sandy and Laura had always been very close. "When you're ready, though. I will definitely come visit you again soon, as long as it's okay with you and Scott."

"You're always welcome here, Mom. Is Aunt Tammy still planning on coming to visit you?"

"Yes." Maddie smiled at the thought of her younger sister visiting. They had always been close, but they hadn't lived in the same town since Maddie had left Bayview almost thirty years ago. They would often make the two-hour drive to visit each other, but they hadn't seen each other for a few months.

"That's good. Oh, Caitlyn's up. I'd better get her. I love you!"

"I love you, too, sweetie. Give her lots of kisses for me."

As Maddie ended the call, her heart sank as her eyes settled on the bay, and she recalled pulling Helen's body from it. How could she ever invite her daughter and granddaughter to visit a place with a murderer on the loose? No, she had to make sure that Bayview was safe before she could allow them to visit. And what would happen when Sandy heard about the murder that took place? If she wasn't so distracted with Caitlyn, she probably would have heard about it already. Maddie could only imagine the worry that Sandy and her siblings would express, if they discovered what had happened.

Maddie finished her tea as she continued to stare at the water. Whether Jake wanted her to be involved or not, whether it was the wisest decision for her to continue to snoop around, she felt as if she had no choice but to help find the truth. If this was to be her home again, she wanted it to be the place she could imagine growing old in. A place where her children and grandchildren could visit, safely, with nothing but good memories to make.

That night, as Maddie sprawled out in bed, under a very familiar roof, she felt the chaos of her life swirl around her. She'd gone from one mess to another. But if she wanted things to ever be normal again, she would have to find a way to make it happen herself. Once Helen's murder was solved, then maybe she could begin to sort the rest out.

Maddie cuddled Bella and Polly closer and finally began to relax. The memory of Helen's voice started playing through her mind. No, she wasn't well loved, but she was a person who had made an impact on Bayview, she was someone who thought she knew what was best. No matter the commotion she caused, it didn't give anyone the right to kill her. Justice had to be served, and she couldn't wait on the police chief to serve it. She would do everything she could to track down Helen's killer, even if that meant alienating Jake even more than she already had.

Maddie finally fell asleep to the soft snores of Bella and Polly.

CHAPTER 19

addie woke the next morning with the thoughts of finding Helen's murderer still on her mind. As she snuggled on the couch with Bella and Polly, she began making a list of suspects. Frances was one, as were the Billings brothers, and though she hesitated to add Peter's name, she scribbled it down just to prove Jake wrong. She wrote down Nancy's name, then skimmed over the list again. If she wanted to continue investigating, she needed to have some kind of system in place.

At the moment, the Billings brothers seemed to be prime suspects. They would benefit the most, if the resort was no longer an option. Then they could build their amusement park and their business could become successful. Not only that, but both had been arrested before, they were not strangers to criminal behavior. She decided that she needed to speak to them in person before she could learn anything else about them.

Maddie pulled out her phone and searched for the address of their office. Once she had it, she decided she would pay them a visit. If she showed up out of the blue, she might catch them off guard, which might lead to them being honest in their answers. She fed the dogs, took them for a walk along the beach, then dropped them off at home and headed for the middle of town.

The Billings brothers had an office in a building that housed a few small shops as well as business offices. She made her way through the building until she came to the correct office. The door was made of frosted glass, and the single window had the blinds lowered and snapped shut. However, she could see light spilling through the crack between the bottom of the door and the floor. Within minutes, she heard voices inside. They were muffled at first, but she could tell there were two, and both were heated.

Maddie stood just outside the door and listened as the aggravated voices began to escalate in volume.

"You put us in this situation with your impulsive decisions, Benjamin! You don't ever think anything through!" She presumed that the deep, strong voice, belonged to the older Billings brother, Bob.

"And if I waited for you to make a decision, we'd still be sitting on the couch in Mom's basement!"

Benjamin's slightly higher pitched voice was just as determined.

"Just keep pointing the finger! It's going to solve everything to blame me, isn't it? Meanwhile, if we don't get this approval today, we're going to lose the entire opportunity, Benjamin!"

"Just try to calm down, Bob!" A sharp sound indicated Benjamin might have hit something. "You're panicking, and that's going to make us look weak! With Helen gone, we don't have any competition. Just keep your head on straight, and we're going to get through this."

"You're right." Bob sighed. "You're right. I'm going to try to calm down. It's just that we have so much riding on this, it's such a risk."

"I told you, there's nothing to worry about. I promised you that I would take care of it, and I did."

The knob on the door began to turn. Maddie took a step back, and in that moment, decided she didn't want to meet the brothers in person just yet. She thought she might be able to learn more by keeping an eye on them. She ducked into a small alcove near a bathroom, just before the younger brother, Benjamin, walked past her.

Maddie waited until she heard the office door close, then stepped out into the hallway. With neither brother in sight, she headed for the door. She stepped out just in time to see Benjamin get into the driver's seat of an old jeep. As he pulled away from the curb, she hurried to her car. She didn't have to follow him far before the jeep pulled to a stop right in front of Frances' flower shop.

Maddie's heart dropped as she wondered if he'd noticed she was following him. He seemed like the type to be suspicious. After all, he'd spent some time behind bars, he had committed crimes. How could she have thought that she would get away with tracking him?

A second later, Benjamin stepped out of the jeep. He looked straight toward her car as she chose a parking spot a few spaces up. Then he turned his attention to the shop. As he started toward it, Frances stepped outside. She smiled as he opened his arms to her.

She embraced him, and within a moment, their lips were locked, and his hands were tangled in her hair.

Maddie took a sharp breath at the sight. Clearly, the two were familiar with each other. Could there have been even more to Helen and Frances' conflict? Could Frances have been working hard to support her boyfriend's business venture, and that caused even more friction between her and Helen? The fact that Helen had broken up her parents' marriage, upset her mother, and stood as a direct competitor to her boyfriend's success, made Frances, Maddie's prime suspect.

With her heart pounding, Maddie waited until the couple broke apart. As she watched, the two exchanged a few words, then Benjamin got back into his jeep and drove away. Frances stared after him for a few moments before turning back toward the shop and stepping inside.

Maddie seized the opportunity to follow right behind her.

"Maddie, right?" Frances glanced over her shoulder and smiled. "Good to see you again."

"You as well." Maddie smiled as she looked over the flowers on display. "I bet everyone loves your flowers."

"I do have my regulars." Frances walked over to a few bouquets still in the midst of being arranged. "Are you looking for something again today?"

"Yes, actually, but not flowers. I'm looking for company." Maddie grinned. "Any chance you'd be willing to join me for lunch?"

"Today?" Frances looked up at her.

"Yes, now, if you're free. I know it's a bit early, but we can call it brunch." Maddie laughed. "I just hate eating alone, and I don't know many people here. I'd love to get to know you better. I've heard such wonderful things about you and your business."

"Really? From who?" Frances smiled.

Maddie's heart skipped a beat as she tried to come up with a name quickly. "Beatrice just raves about you."

"Oh, that's because of the roses." Frances laughed,

then nodded. "I always keep her favorite roses in stock."

"Does she buy them often?" Maddie paused in front of the fresh bouquets and leaned in to sniff their fragrance.

"Not ever, actually. However, Helen would come in to buy them when Beatrice would come for a visit. I guess it was her way of trying to prove she was a good daughter-in-law. Or maybe there was another reason." Frances shrugged. "Either way, I guess it won't be happening anymore."

Maddie's jaw tensed as she recalled Benjamin with his arms around Frances. Had the lovebirds worked together to ensure that Helen would no longer be a problem for them?

"I guess not." She frowned. "So, what do you think? Can we share some lunch?"

"Sure, I have someone who can cover the shop for a little while. I'd love to hear more about the bakery your parents ran. I'm curious about all of the old businesses around here." Frances took off her apron, then signaled to a young woman behind the counter. "I won't be long. Can you finish the bouquets for me? They just need some baby's breath."

"Okay, no problem." The young woman nodded.

"Is Janet's okay?" Maddie held the door open for her.

"Is there anywhere else?" Frances laughed. "If she ever closes, we'll all starve."

"Good point." Maddie grinned.

"I know it's not a long walk, but I can't be very long." Frances gestured to her car.

"I'll meet you over there."

As Maddie drove along the harbor toward the restaurant, she passed the large building that had once housed her parents' bakery. It had sat empty for so many years that she wondered what it might look like inside. She knew that it was another thing she would have to face, but at the moment she had other things on her mind.

CHAPTER 20

*O*nce settled at their table, Maddie focused her attention on the young woman across from her.

"I noticed you earlier with Benjamin Billings."

"Oh?" Frances' cheeks flushed.

"Have you two been dating long?" Maddie took a sip of her water.

"What makes you think we're dating?" Frances narrowed her eyes.

"I saw you two kissing." Maddie shrugged. "I know that doesn't always mean much these days, but you looked so close, so happy to see each other. I'm sure that Helen wasn't too pleased with the relationship."

Frances frowned. "Today was the first day we felt comfortable kissing in public. It still makes me a little nervous, to be honest."

"Because Helen would have been furious, if she found out?" Maddie sat back as the waitress brought her salad. She frowned as she wished that there were fries to put on top.

"So, this wasn't an invitation to lunch, was it? This was a trap?" Frances locked her eyes to Maddie's, heat darkening the light brown shade. "I thought you wanted to get to know me better, but you're just digging for dirt?"

"It's not a trap, Frances." Maddie stretched her hand across the table and rested it beside Frances'. "I thought we could discuss some things that might come up for you. I went to visit your mother, and after speaking with her, I get the feeling that you don't have too many people to turn to."

"You went to visit her?" Frances drew her hand back and frowned. "Why did you really invite me to lunch? Are you trying to prove I was involved in Helen's murder somehow?"

"No, not at all. I'm trying to help you. You have to admit that there was bad blood between you and Helen. Now, you're making it public that you're with Benjamin Billings, who was practically in direct competition with Helen." Maddie scrutinized the younger woman's expression. "Your mom cares about you so much and I just wanted to see if I could help guide you through this. How long have you been seeing Benjamin?"

"We've been together for a little over a year."

Frances brushed her hair back from her eyes as she leaned closer to Maddie. "We had to keep our relationship a secret because I knew that if Helen caught wind of it, she would do everything in her power to destroy my shop and ruin my life, again. I just couldn't let that happen."

"It sounds a little extreme to believe she would react so harshly, all over a business deal." Maddie shook her head. "Isn't it possible that she wouldn't have cared much at all?"

"Ask people in this town whether they would prefer to have the resort or the amusement park, and they will tell you the amusement park. A few days ago, they would have told you the resort. That's how much power Helen had over the people in this town. She didn't just drum up support, she bulldozed anyone who opposed it. People around here, they're not wealthy, they can't risk a blow to their businesses or finances. She knew that, and she took advantage of it."

"That sounds terrible." Maddie met her eyes.

"It was." Frances' phone beeped and she took it out of her pocket. She stood up from the table, her sandwich not even touched. "I'm sorry, there's a problem with a flower delivery, we'll have to catch up another time. You need to be careful, Maddie. You may think you know everything there is to know about the people in this town but it's not the same place you left so long ago. Enjoy your food." She smiled as she turned and walked out of the restaurant.

Maddie stared after her, disappointed that she hadn't had the opportunity to speak to her more.

"Poor girl." Janet sighed as she walked over to Maddie's table. "She seems upset again. At least she's not as upset as she was the last time she was here." She shook her head as she picked up Maddie's water glass to fill it.

"She was upset the last time she was here?" Maddie met her eyes as she set the glass down in front of her.

"Yes. It was the day Helen died. Someone received a text about it, and the news spread across the restaurant. As soon as she and her friend, really her boyfriend, Benjamin Billings, no one can keep a secret from me, heard about the murder, they both bolted. They hadn't even started their lunch and didn't ask to take it with them. Just like today." Janet gestured to the sandwich. "Do you want to have it with your salad?"

"Yes. Why not?" Maddie pulled the plate across the table.

"People are a little sensitive right now." Janet frowned. "Oh Maddie, I do believe I'm getting too old for this job. When are you going to open your parents' bakery, so I can open later?"

"Ha, very funny." Maddie shook her head.

"We'll see." Janet winked at her, then turned and walked away.

For a moment Maddie's mind filled with thoughts

of reopening the bakery. She'd spent so much of her time there when she was young. She started out by drawing pictures on the chalkboard that listed the specials, then ended up working behind the counter and helping out in the kitchen, before she moved away. It had been a second home to her. But it had never occurred to her it could be a new career.

The truth was, she didn't have the money to invest in opening. Although she loved baking, she wasn't experienced enough in baking to keep up with it. She would have to hire at least one baker. She pushed the thought away and focused her attention back on Frances.

If what Janet said was true and she and Benjamin had been at the restaurant on the day of Helen's murder, then there was a good chance they both had a solid alibi. However, she couldn't know that, without knowing the exact time of Helen's death. There was only one way to find that out.

Maddie polished off the sandwich, took a few bites of her salad, then left the payment for the food and a generous tip. On her way out the door she waved to Janet, who winked at her again.

"Not happening, Janet!" She pulled the door closed behind her.

Maddie pulled out Jake's card and tried calling his number. She wanted to speak to him about Frances and wasn't sure if he was at the station. The phone just went to voicemail and she didn't leave a message. She decided she would go to the station and see if he was there. If he wasn't, someone else might be willing to talk to her about the case and offer up some information.

As Maddie drove to the police station, she noticed that the people in town had mostly gotten back to normal. All of the businesses were active. People walked along the sidewalks. No one seemed to be frightened by the idea of a killer loose in town. She guessed that was because they all assumed that Helen had been killed for a specific reason, and that not everyone was a potential victim. But what if they were wrong? What if Helen's death hadn't been personal at all?

The thought set her nerves on edge. If she didn't find out some real information soon, she wondered if she would begin to suspect everyone that she set eyes on.

CHAPTER 21

*M*addie stepped into the police station and glanced around for the first friendly face. The police officer at the front desk smiled at her as she approached.

"I need to speak to someone about the investigation into Helen's murder, please." She looked into the officer's eyes.

"Don't worry about it, Sawyer, I'll take care of this." Jake stepped up to the front desk. His gaze settled on Maddie the moment she turned to look at him.

"Jake, great. I have some questions I hope you can answer." Maddie smiled, hoping to ease the hint of tension that she already sensed between them.

"Why don't we step over here?" Jake gestured to a sitting area not far from the desk. "I'm surprised to see you here."

"I'm just curious about something." Maddie sat down in one of the chairs. Though she expected him to do the same, he remained standing.

"Even though I've suggested it's not such a good idea to snoop around?" Jake frowned, his eyes sharp as they assessed her.

"Jake, do we really need to go over that again?" Maddie sighed. "Listen, I might have some important information for you. I just need to know the exact time of Helen's death, and you might be able to rule out a couple of suspects."

"Oh?" Jake eased down into the chair beside her. "Which suspects?"

"Frances, and her secret boyfriend, Benjamin Billings." Maddie met his eyes, determined to see the surprise she expected him to experience at that revelation.

"We already know about those two." Jake shook his head. "But how you came upon that information, I'm pretty curious about."

"Never mind that. The point is, they were at Janet's around the time Helen was killed, and if it was at the time she was killed, then neither of them was involved, right?" Maddie tapped her fingertips against the arm of the chair that separated them. "So, I just need to know the time of death, that's all."

"You just want to know information about a crime, that you have no right to know?" Jake raised his eyebrows, then looked up at the ceiling. "Maddie, we already know they have an alibi. They have been ruled out as suspects. They're not who I'm interested in finding out more information about."

"Then who?" Maddie asked.

"There's one person who doesn't have an alibi, has plenty of motive, and refuses to speak to me." Jake looked over at her. "Peter."

"Not Peter." Maddie shook her head. "He wasn't involved in any of this."

"You don't know that for sure." Jake frowned.

"I just know he could never do this." Maddie shrugged.

"If you have so much faith in him, then maybe you can help me prove his innocence." Jake's eyes lingered on hers, as his tone became more professional.

"How can I do that?" Maddie stared back at him, uncertain about his intentions.

"You two are such good friends, I imagine you could get yourself invited into his home. If so, I'd like you to do that for me. For us both. Get an invite, and I'll just happen to show up with you. I can have a look around, feel things out." A soft smile crossed Jake's lips. "If he has nothing to hide, there shouldn't be anything to find, right?"

"You want me to trick my friend into having his home searched by you?" Maddie gave a short laugh. "I don't think so."

"So, you don't think he's as innocent as you

claim?" Jake folded his thick arms across his chest as he studied her.

"I don't think it's right to betray my friend, just to satisfy your suspicion." Maddie stood up from her chair.

"You'd rather protect a potential killer than betray your friendship?" Jake stared up at her.

"I don't think he's a killer. I won't betray him." Maddie winced. "Betrayal causes so much damage but we're never fully aware of the amount of damage it can do."

"I'll try to keep that in mind." Jake nodded to her as she walked toward the door. "Be careful, Maddie."

"Always." Maddie let the door swing closed behind her. She decided, if he wasn't going to be of any help to her, then she would just have to come across more information in other ways. It was clear to her that he was after Peter, and he would be looking for evidence to prove his suspicions. Maybe she could protect her friend and solve the murder at the same time, by finding out exactly what Helen was up to on the day she was killed.

Maddie headed back to the central location for all gossip in Bayview, Janet's Place. When she stepped inside, she found Janet's young waitress, Lacy, at the counter.

"Back for a second lunch?" Lacy grinned as she leaned against the counter. "Or an extra thick milkshake?"

"Actually, just for a little information." Maddie ignored her body's reaction to the mention of a milkshake. Now wasn't the time for a sugar buzz. "You were working the day that Helen was killed, right?"

"Yes." Lacy frowned. "I try not to think too much about it."

"I don't want you to think too much about what happened to her, but did you hear anything about her that day? About where she might have been? I just want to find out what she was up to that day, if I can." Maddie glanced around the dining room. If she went through her activities that day, she might be able to unearth some other suspects. But the hard part was going to be pinpointing where she was and what she was up to.

"Honestly, I don't think that will be too hard to find out." Lacy smiled some. "Helen was not a quiet person. She made a show everywhere she went, so I think you'll find it's pretty easy to track her movements. I can get you started. She came into the restaurant when you and Amber were here. Then she came in a bit later for a coffee. She got it to go, because she intended to head over to town hall."

"That's a great start, Lacy, thank you so much." Maddie left a few dollars for a tip, then headed back out of the restaurant. She was almost to her car, when Amber waved to her from farther down the sidewalk.

CHAPTER 22

"*M*addie! What are you up to?" Amber rolled her eyes as she paused in front of her. "Never mind, I know what you're up to. Trying to be a crime solver, right?"

"Right." Maddie glanced down the street. "I feel so strange digging into Helen's life like this. She's the victim, but somehow I'm treating her more like the criminal."

"She's the victim for sure." Amber crossed her arms. "But she wasn't exactly innocent. Maybe her crimes didn't warrant her death, but she certainly committed them."

"Is that how you really feel, Amber?" Maddie frowned.

"I just don't want you to be surprised, if the deeper you dig, the dirtier she gets." Amber narrowed her eyes, then lowered her voice. "There were even rumors at one point that she killed Chuck. I'm not saying that's true, there was never any proof of it, but I honestly wouldn't put it past her."

"Wow." Maddie took a step back as her mind swirled with the new information. What if Helen had killed Chuck? What would that change? "But the medical examiner never found anything suspicious?"

"As far as I know an exam wasn't done. It was deemed natural causes. Like I said, he had been having some heart problems." Amber shook her head. "There was no reason to suspect anything else."

"But people did?" Maddie looked into Amber's eyes. "Why? Just because she wasn't a nice person?"

"Yes, I think so. I did hear rumors that Chuck and Helen had a disagreement over something to do with the surf shop in the last few weeks of Chuck's life. I don't know any details, though." Amber winced, then met Maddie's eyes again. "I really don't like dealing with rumors, but I just didn't want you to go into this blind. Many people have strong feelings about Helen around here, and most of them are not pleasant."

"I see, thanks for the heads-up." Maddie squeezed her shoulder. "Don't worry, I am going to get to the bottom of this, then we can have the kind of reunion we were meant to."

"Oh?" Amber's eyes glistened as she gazed back at her. "Are you going to invite Jake?"

"Jake?" Maddie laughed.

"He's one of the most eligible bachelors in town,

and you've already snagged him!" Amber huffed with a fake pout. "It's not fair."

"Oh stop." Maddie laughed again and gave her friend a playful shove. "It's not like that at all."

"Oh, you might be able to convince someone else of that. But I saw how happy he was when he heard you were coming back to Bayview." Amber raised her eyebrows, then shrugged. "Why not go for it? What harm could it do?"

"I'm nowhere near ready for anything like that." Maddie tipped her head to the side as she looked her over. "What about you? When are you going to get back out there?"

"Oh, I'm out there already." Amber grinned. "I'd better get to the store, have I mentioned that I hate my boss?"

"That doesn't sound like fun." Maddie gave her a quick hug.

"It's not, but it passes the time working at the grocery store. And I do love talking to the customers." Amber continued past her down the sidewalk.

Maddie drove toward town hall. She noticed a familiar crowd of protesters gathered there. However, today they didn't hold any signs. As she stepped out of her car, she searched for Peter among the crowd. Not seeing him, she walked over to a woman just outside of the gathering.

"What's happening here?"

"We're continuing to protest the possibility of the

resort being built in town, but with Helen gone, it's really just to make sure our voices are still heard." She smiled. "Isn't it a relief not to have to worry so much?"

"I guess protesting with Helen around wasn't easy. Were you here the day she died?" Maddie again looked through the crowd for Peter.

"Do you mean the day that she tried to have us all arrested?" She laughed. "Oh yeah, I was here. She and Peter nearly came to blows. I've never seen him that angry before. She kept dialing her phone, saying she was going to personally have Chief Holden arrest us all." She shook her head. "She wanted us to believe that she had him in her pocket. Chief Holden may be a lot of things, but he's never been bought by anyone. None of us believed her."

"Did he show up?" Maddie asked.

"Yes, but he actually asked her to leave, insisted on it. He even insisted on escorting her home, and made her promise she would stay there, otherwise she would end up in handcuffs." She frowned. "I guess it's not so amusing now, but at the time, it was pretty funny to watch. She was so upset."

"Interesting." Maddie looked back toward the crowd. "So, where's Peter today?"

"I don't know. He's usually always here. I guess he just didn't make it today." She shrugged, then walked off into the crowd.

If Helen really did go back home, then maybe Nancy will remember seeing her. Maddie walked back to her car and drove in the direction of Helen's house. She pulled into Nancy's driveway and hoped that she would be alone. With only one car parked near the bungalow, she crossed her fingers. She hoped that she would get more information from her without Max there.

She barely had a chance to knock on the door before it swung open.

"Maddie." Nancy smiled. "I was just about to work in the garden."

"Do you mind if I join you?" Maddie followed her around to the side garden.

"No, I don't mind, but if you're here, you're pulling weeds." Nancy pointed to the weeds growing around the flowers in her garden. "I've been too distracted to keep up with them, with everything that's been going on."

"That's actually why I'm here." Maddie lowered herself down to her knees and began to pluck the weeds from the soil. "I was wondering if you saw Helen at home on the day she died."

"I saw her car." Nancy frowned. "I can't say that I saw her, though. I was trying to catch up with her that day, but I didn't want to go to her house. I didn't want to upset her more. I was hoping to run into her."

"I see." Maddie pulled a few more weeds. "Did you notice Helen often walking down by the water?" She moved on to the next section of the garden.

"Helen?" Nancy shook her head as she pulled up

handfuls of weeds. "No, she never went down there. She was always worried about her outfits and didn't like to get near anything she thought might be dirty. She never wanted to risk getting wet."

"So, you never saw her at all?" Maddie looked over her shoulder, down toward Helen's property. "Not even out on the dock?" She pointed out the large, wooden, white dock that stretched out from the rear of the property.

"It's beautiful, isn't it?" Nancy looked over at it as well. "Chuck built it. But no, I never saw Helen down there. Chuck's mother, Beatrice, would come over to go out on the boat with him or fish with him from the dock. That was the only time that Helen would go down there. She'd go just far enough to hand over drinks and snacks to them."

"She must have really wanted to make a good impression on her mother-in-law, if she risked getting her clothes dirty to bring her refreshments." Maddie turned to face her.

"Oh, no I don't think that's the case." Nancy laughed. "Helen pretended to be nice to Beatrice for Chuck's sake. She would buy her roses, but really Helen and Beatrice did not get along well at all. In fact, not long before Chuck died, I overheard a fierce argument between himself and his mother. She wanted Chuck to leave Helen. She said that Helen had him trapped and that he should leave her."

"Wow, that must have been quite an argument. But did Chuck agree with her? Did he feel trapped?"

"He insisted that he wasn't going anywhere, and when she pushed, he said that he had promised to stay with her for life." Nancy stood up and dusted off her gloves. "I remember thinking that he was a sweet and loyal man. Never did it cross my mind that he could be in danger."

"So, you believe that Helen may have had something to do with his death?" Maddie took a sharp breath as she recalled Amber's mention of the same thing. "Are you sure about that?"

"No, I can't be sure. On the surface it looked like an unfortunate death, no one to blame. But the way Helen was—" Nancy gritted her teeth, then shook her head. "The first time I heard Beatrice accuse her of it, something clicked in me. I could see it. I couldn't figure out how she did it, or whether it was true, but I could picture it. Helen just didn't like to be challenged, she didn't like anyone else making decisions that affected her."

"You heard Beatrice accuse Helen of killing her son?" Maddie stood up as well and wiped her hands on her jeans. "When was this?"

"It happened more than one time, actually. I can't recall exactly when." Nancy frowned.

"Recently?" Maddie searched Nancy's eyes.

"No, it wasn't recent. At least not in the past month or so."

"Interesting." Maddie nodded. "It sounds like there was no love lost between the two of them."

"Beatrice has never been an easy woman herself. So, maybe they were just too similar."

"That's true." Maddie could recall Beatrice's sharp tone as she spoke to her son, and any playmates that he'd gathered in their vast yard. She didn't like to be bothered, but in general she tended to leave the kids alone. She would often spend time inside with her sister, Shirley, and when things got too loud, Beatrice would emerge from the house with a shout that sent them all scattering. While she was a generous woman, she was never to be crossed. If she really believed that Helen might have been involved in her only son's death, she could only imagine her fury.

CHAPTER 23

*A*fter leaving Nancy's house, Maddie's thoughts still centered around Beatrice and the possibility that she suspected Helen of her son's murder. When Chuck was a boy, Beatrice would have done anything to protect him. She could only guess that her desire to keep him safe had become even more obsessive as he entered into a relationship with a woman that she couldn't stand.

After taking Bella and Polly for a long walk, she returned to the house and decided that she needed some expert opinions on the situation. She invited Amber and Iris over for coffee. As she prepared the coffee and placed the chocolate cupcakes she hadn't taken to Beatrice on a plate, she tried to picture Beatrice and Helen alone together. Would Beatrice really decide to attack Helen? If she had truly believed that Helen killed Chuck, why hadn't she killed her right after he died? Why would she have waited so long?

Maddie set the plate on the table outside, just as Amber pulled into the driveway. She and her mother greeted the dogs as they stepped up onto the porch.

"Thanks for inviting us." Amber smiled. "I knocked off work early, and mother was bored with her knitting."

"I don't knit!" Iris huffed. "Amber just thinks I should."

"It's a safer hobby than waterskiing." Amber flopped down into one of the chairs at the table and picked up a cupcake. "You need to start thinking about slowing down!"

"Child," Iris snapped as she sat down beside her.

"Sorry." Amber frowned.

"You two." Maddie laughed as she sat down across from them. "There's not much I missed more about Bayview than the two of you."

"We're such a treat." Amber had a bite of the cupcake. "These are so good. I miss your cupcakes."

"Listen, I have something I want to ask you both. I don't want this to go anywhere further than this table, okay?" Maddie looked between the two of them.

"You can trust us, Maddie, you know that." Amber had a sip of coffee. "What is it?"

"Do you think that Beatrice might be capable of murder?" Maddie winced as she spoke the words.

"Now, you suspect Beatrice?" Amber's eyes widened. "She's over seventy."

"I know." Maddie held up her hands. "But that doesn't mean anything really. She's always been strong. She certainly doesn't look or act her age. I don't think I can rule her out just because of her age."

"I wouldn't." Iris spoke up. "Beatrice has always been capable of getting whatever it is she wants. She loved her son, and that was about it."

"Loved him enough to kill, if she thought Helen had something to do with his death?" Maddie met Iris' eyes.

"Oh, dear." Iris sighed. "That's just a rumor."

"A rumor, that I have good reason to believe Beatrice thinks is true." Maddie glanced at Amber, then looked back at Iris. "Nancy said she overheard Beatrice accusing Helen of killing Chuck."

"What?" Amber gasped. "I had no idea she actually accused her!"

"That's terrible." Iris shook her head. "I had no love for Helen, but she shouldn't have had to endure those kinds of accusations."

"So, you don't think there's any truth to them?" Maddie sat back in her chair.

"Not a trace of truth." Iris slapped her knee.

"Mom, are you sure?" Amber looked over at her.

"Pretty sure. All I heard was that he had a heart attack. That was that." Iris brushed her palms together. "But if Beatrice got it into her head that

Helen had something to do with it, oh I can't even imagine what Helen's life might have been like after that."

An engine drew their attention to the driveway. Peter's car pulled up on the other side of Maddie's car.

"Is that Peter?" Iris squinted at the driveway.

"Yes, it is, I forgot he was coming over." Maddie winced as she recalled that he was having dinner with her. In all her travels, she had yet to get back to the grocery store to buy something for dinner.

"Let's go, Amber." Iris finished her coffee, then stood up.

"Mom, please, it's fine." Amber stood up as well.

"No, we should leave." Iris grabbed her daughter's hand and tugged her down the steps.

"Is something wrong?" Maddie followed them down the steps as Peter walked toward her.

"Amber." Peter froze as he met her eyes. "I didn't know you'd be here."

"We're just leaving." Amber steered her mother to her car. "I'll catch up with you later." She smiled at Peter.

"It's good to see you, Iris." Peter took a step toward her.

Iris didn't reply or look at him as she settled in the passenger seat.

Seconds later, Amber's car backed down the driveway.

"What was that all about?" Maddie walked up the porch steps.

"Not sure." Peter followed after her onto the porch, where Bella and Polly attacked him with licks and nuzzles.

"But you must have some idea?" Maddie walked through the house, with Peter and the dogs following. "Iris is one of the kindest people I know."

"She's not fond of me." Peter placed a loaf of rye bread on the kitchen counter. "I don't know why."

"What about Helen? You two had a few run-ins, too, didn't you?" Maddie met his eyes.

"I made it my business to stay out of her way as much as possible. She made it her business to confront me any chance she got. You have to try this bread." Peter grabbed a knife from a stand as he took the bread out of the container and put it on a board. He glanced back at her. "What's with all of the questions?"

"Sorry, I'm just trying to figure some things out. It always helps me to talk things through." Maddie walked slowly back and forth behind him as she considered his words. "So, she was always seeking you out? Trying to bait you into a fight?" She could imagine this scenario playing out in a way that ended up with Helen dead. But could she believe it was true?

"She was good at that, yes." Peter glanced over at her.

"I'm sure that she got under your skin, huh?" Maddie smiled as she paused behind him.

"I don't know, I didn't pay that much attention." Peter cleared his throat.

"Except on the day she died. You paid a lot of attention, didn't you?" Maddie tried to keep her voice relaxed. "You were really angry."

Peter swung around suddenly, his eyes sharp as they landed on hers.

"How many different ways are you going to ask me if I killed her, Maddie? I thought we already went over this!" His voice raised with every word he spoke, and his grip tightened on the knife in his hand.

Maddie took a quick step back. Her eyes widened with fear as she watched his anger ripple through him, from the tension in his muscles, to the rough edge of his voice.

CHAPTER 24

"*I*'m sorry, Peter, I didn't mean to upset you." In all the time she'd known him as a kid, Maddie couldn't recall a moment that he'd lost his temper with her.

Maddie's heart pounded as she wondered if she'd just walked into the exact situation that Jake warned her about. Had she pushed too far and brought out the killer in Peter?

Peter sighed and closed his eyes. "No, I'm the one that should be sorry." He shook his head as he looked back at her. "I'm so sorry, Maddie. I shouldn't have spoken to you like that. My temper has been short lately, with all the protests going on, and the possibility of losing my house, and now Helen's death. It's not like I don't know that I'm Chief Holden's prime suspect." He winced and set the knife down on the counter beside him. "Maddie, please, don't be frightened. I would never do anything to hurt you."

"Never?" Maddie stared straight into his eyes. "Maybe you wouldn't hurt me, but with that short temper, I can only imagine how difficult it would be to resist hurting Helen."

"No!" Peter's voice echoed through the house as he narrowed his eyes. "No, I would never do that! Maddie, I don't care what the rest of this town believes, but you have to hear me when I say this. I may have been angry at Helen, I may have hoped that she would just disappear. But I never hurt her, and I never would. You know me, you know that." He frowned. "Even after all these years, you don't really believe I could do it, do you?"

"There was a time when I knew how to answer a question like that." Maddie studied him. She could easily see the boy she'd hung around as often as possible as a girl. It seemed as if decades vanished, and she was a young girl with a crush. "But I've learned that even people I considered to be trustworthy can lie right to my face, and I won't know the difference."

"I'm not lying." Peter tapped his chest. "You know my heart, Maddie, I know you do."

"Peter." Maddie wanted to believe him, but he certainly seemed angry enough to kill Helen. "All I want to know is the truth. All I want to know is what happened to Helen. There's an easy way to prove you

162

had nothing do to with Helen's murder. Where were you when she was murdered?"

"You want to know where I was when Helen was killed?" Peter met her eyes. "If you want to know that truth, then you should ask Amber about it." His phone beeped. He took it out of his pocket and frowned when he looked at it. "Sorry, I have to get going. I forgot my weekly card game has been changed to tonight and it's at my house. We'll have dinner another night?"

"Of course." Maddie watched him leave. As much as she wanted to believe he had nothing to do with Helen's murder, she still wasn't convinced. She pulled out her phone to call Amber.

"Amber, I need you to come back, if you can please? I need to talk to you."

"Of course, I'll be right there," Amber replied without hesitation.

Minutes after Maddie ended the call, she spotted Amber's car pulling into the driveway.

"Is everything okay?" Amber bounded up the steps as the two dogs raced up to greet her. She bent down to pat their heads.

"Yes, thank you for coming over. I'm trying to sort all of this out." Maddie began to pace back and forth. The dogs followed her with their eyes.

"Are you going to tell me what this is all about?" Amber leaned against the post as she watched her pace.

"When Peter was here earlier, he said some things that I'm not sure whether to believe." Maddie turned around to look at her friend.

"Peter's a pretty trustworthy guy. But I bet I don't have to tell you that." Amber flashed a smile at her. "You remember."

"I remember having a crush on an older boy that didn't even know I existed." Maddie rolled her eyes as she leaned back against the door. "That certainly doesn't mean that I know him now."

"Maybe not, but I'd bet that you have a pretty good idea of who he really is, as you spent quite a bit of time with him in the bakery." Amber grinned.

"Maybe. But he seemed to think that I'd get more information from you." Maddie met her eyes. "Especially about where he was when Helen was killed?"

"Oh." Amber winced as she glanced away from her. "Right."

"Right?" Maddie raised her eyebrows.

"He was at my house." Amber nodded. "We've been spending some time together lately."

"Amber." Maddie smiled. "Why didn't you say something? That's great."

"Because we've only been out a couple of times." Amber looked down at her hands. "We're just taking things slowly. We're really more like close friends."

"I'm sorry, Amber." Maddie shook her head. "I didn't realize. I should have, though. I've been so distracted with all of this, I'm still not being a very good friend."

"You're a great friend, Maddie." Amber took her hand and looked into her eyes. "The truth is, Peter and I had a late lunch at my place, then he went to put some shelving up in the garage for me. I was so tired because I couldn't sleep the night before and I've been working long hours, so I fell asleep on the couch. I woke up when I heard all of the sirens. When I did, he was gone. But to tell you the truth, I have no idea when he actually left. I've been avoiding Jake's questions because I can't really give Peter an alibi." She frowned. "I know how it looks, but I really don't think Peter could do something like this."

"Why does your mother have a problem with him?" Maddie asked.

"She thinks he should become more serious about our relationship." Amber rolled her eyes. "She blames him and thinks he's just stringing me along, but she doesn't understand that I like things the way they are. She's always meddling."

CHAPTER 25

*M*addie watched Amber pull out of the driveway. As she processed the news that Amber and Peter had started dating, she was even more determined to find out if Peter was involved in the murder.

Eager to help get to the truth, she decided to pay a visit to Jake at the police station. She needed more information, and he was her best source. She just hoped that he would be willing to share.

She walked into the living room and saw Bella and Polly curled up together in a dog bed. They each had their own, but they always ended up together in the same bed.

"I won't be long." Maddie patted their heads, then walked out of the house and headed to the police station.

When Maddie arrived, she found Jake talking to an officer at the front desk.

"Jake?" Maddie called out as he started to walk toward the back.

"Maddie." Jake turned to look at her with a faint sigh. "Why am I not surprised?"

"Do you have a minute?" Maddie smiled.

"Sure." Jake nodded. "Come to my office."

He directed her down the hallway and through an office door. He walked around the desk and sat down. He gestured for her to sit on the chair in front of his desk.

The files piled up on his desk were thick, and she noticed that one in particular was spread open in front of his chair.

"What can I do for you?" Jake's gaze remained on her.

"Is there anything more you can tell me about the investigation?" Maddie settled in the chair. "I'm really having a hard time right now, knowing what to believe, who to believe. I'm hoping you can give me some kind of direction."

"Funny, I was hoping you would do the same." Jake smiled some as he looked into her eyes, then glanced down at the file on his desk. "There have been plenty of twists and turns in this investigation."

"What if I told you that Peter has an alibi, at least a partial one?" Maddie smiled.

"There's no such thing as a partial alibi." Jake shook his head.

"It's better than nothing." Maddie told Jake about Peter's alibi.

"That's not exactly airtight, is it?" Jake frowned. "Did he tell you anything else?"

"No." Maddie bit into her bottom lip as she wondered if she should admit that he might have been right about her not being safe alone with him. "Can you tell me anything new?"

"We believe that Helen was killed by the section of the bay near her house." Jake looked up from the file on his desk. "Not too many people know that. We thought that keeping the location of the murder out of the press might help us with the investigation. So far, it hasn't really turned up any new leads. We had suspected it from the get-go. Now, with the medical examiner's findings and some further investigation from local scientists, we are confident that she was killed there."

"You're keeping it out of the press, but you're telling me?" Maddie's eyes widened some as she noticed the softness in his expression. She expected a lecture, but instead he set his pen down and gazed into her eyes.

"We're planning to release it to the press later today." Jake nodded. "I should warn you to stay out of this investigation. I should ask you to stop digging into things that are police business. But I've watched your dedication and determination through all of this, and I have to say that I admire it. You came back to a town that was no longer your home and you made it your business to help keep it safe." He shook his head, then sat back in his chair. "I realize that no matter what I say, you aren't going to stop until we find out the truth."

"I do want to know what happened to her." Maddie nodded.

"And I admire that. However, I do have to caution you that Helen's killer is still out there. It's easy to assume that only the most suspicious people are capable of murder, but the truth is, everyone, including the person right in front of you right now, is capable of murder. All it takes is the right set of circumstances to push someone over a line they thought it would never be possible to cross. So please, don't just assume you are safe with others."

"Like Peter?" Maddie frowned. "Is that what you're saying?"

"Like anyone, Maddie." Jake sat forward, his eyes narrowed. "You need to grasp the amount of risk you are taking when you talk to anyone that you think might be involved in this murder. I genuinely believe that you want to help the investigation, and I know you won't stay out of this. I've always admired your determination, and that's no different in this situation. Just promise me, you'll be careful."

"I will be." Maddie gazed back into his eyes,

startled by the mixture of compliments and warnings he offered. She wasn't sure whether to feel flattered or frightened by his words. Maybe a little of both. "Did you discover anything else?"

"Not really. There was no evidence to find at the crime scene. She had a head wound, so she might have been hit with something, and she was strangled, but we don't know what with. There were no footprints because of the tide and wind. There was nothing but sand, and grass. Some of the grass was trampled but that could have happened at any time. We believe she was killed near there, because she had last been known to be at her home, and the current of the water would sweep her down to the area of the bay where you found her. Based on the medical examiner's estimate of how long she was in the water, it's our best guess that she came from that location." Jake rubbed his hands together as he sat back in his chair. "The medical examiner has to do more tests. It's still an estimate. We have ruled out Frances and her boyfriend. But if the timeline were to change slightly, they could easily be suspects again."

"What do you think?" Maddie looked into his eyes. "What do your instincts tell you?"

"My instincts tell me that Helen likely knew her killer and felt comfortable enough to walk down to the water with the person." Jake raised an eyebrow. "It's not much, but it's what we have to go on right now."

"Thank you for sharing that with me, Jake."

Maddie recalled Amber's insistence that he was excited about her move back home and searched his eyes for just a moment longer. However, she found no trace of excitement in his stern gaze.

"Don't make me regret it, Maddie." Jake frowned as he continued to study her. "I don't want to think that something I shared with you led to you getting hurt, or worse. Okay?"

"Okay." Maddie took a breath as the reality of the situation struck her. As much as she wanted to find the truth, Jake looked at things through different eyes. He saw the danger she placed herself in. Amber had mentioned that this might be the only murder he had ever investigated, but from his determination to protect her she guessed that maybe it wasn't.

CHAPTER 26

$\mathcal{W}$anting to find out what might have happened shortly before Helen was murdered, Maddie headed back to her house. She parked on the street, then walked around the side of the house. The afternoon light had begun to fade, but there was enough of it left to illuminate the path that led to the beautiful dock that Chuck had built. It didn't surprise her that he had created something so intricate. He was always the tinkerer of their group of friends. He took time on projects, even when his friends would push him to skip steps in a rush to get it done. On the other side of the dock, was a small area of open sand that ran along the bay. Tall grass grew up in the sand, shielding the space from view.

Drawn to the area, Maddie stepped down off the dock and walked along the sand. She noticed some grass trampled into the wet sand as Jake had described. However, as he had mentioned, there was no other sign of a struggle. She heard the subtle sound of the boat in the water knocking against the side of the dock, but other than that everything was silent. Helen had been there, but she hadn't been alone. Why had she gone down to the water, when it was one of her least favorite places to go? What had drawn her down there? Who had forced her down there?

Maddie closed her eyes and tried to imagine Peter near the water's edge with Helen. Despite the reasons she had to suspect him, she couldn't picture any reason that Helen would agree to go near the edge of the water with him. The pair were not friendly, and despite Helen's bold behavior, she doubted that she would feel safe alone with Peter, considering the conflict between them. If he had forced her down to the water, wouldn't Nancy have heard some kind of commotion? So, if not Peter, then who?

Maybe Benjamin Billings? Again, she couldn't picture a scenario where Helen would willingly go down to the water with him. What about Nancy? She looked up toward the bungalow, where Nancy lived. She hadn't really considered Nancy a strong suspect until that moment. Maybe she had talked Helen into taking a walk with her by the water? Maybe Nancy's opposition to the resort, had led to an argument that led to her killing Helen?

"None of this is right." Maddie sighed as she wiped her hands across her face. When her hands fell back to her sides and her eyes fluttered open, she caught sight of something that stood out against the sand. A bright red petal caught between some grass. Her heart skipped a beat as she realized that never in her entire time of living in Bayview had she seen a flower of that color near the water. She would have noticed something so bright. She took a few steps closer to the grass. The wind rustled through the grass and revealed a few more petals tangled deeper in the tuft of grass.

Maddie's heartbeat quickened as she recalled Frances mentioning the red roses to her.

"Maddie?" A soft voice called out her name from just behind her.

She turned to find Beatrice with a paddle in her hand.

"Beatrice!" Maddie took a step back and felt water soak through her shoe and dampen her sock. Her heart raced as she stared at the woman. Had Helen been standing there gazing at her mother-in-law, with the paddle in her hand, shortly before her death?

Had it happened just like that? Her heart lurched at the thought and she found it hard to take a breath.

"Darling, are you alright?" Beatrice frowned as she leaned the paddle against the side of the dock. "I didn't know anyone was down here. I thought I'd go out for a boat ride, it's such nice weather and there is still a little time before the sun sets."

"Yes, I'm fine," Maddie stumbled over her words

as she realized that Beatrice might not have any idea that she suspected her. She'd grown up with this woman's watchful eye on her. Could she really believe that Beatrice had killed her daughter-in-law? As much as she didn't want to believe it, the more she thought about it, the more sense it made. "I just came down here to take a look around. I've heard so much about the dock that Chuck built, and I wanted to see for myself."

"It's spectacular, isn't it?" Beatrice ran her fingertips along the smooth wood. "That's why I still come out here. I feel like some part of Chuck still lives on in all the hard work he put into this. That probably makes me sound a little crazy." She smiled as she looked back at Maddie.

Maddie swallowed hard as she noted the grief in Beatrice's eyes. Did she really believe that Helen had killed Chuck? If she did, then she could have easily felt justified in killing Helen.

"Do join me for a boat ride, won't you?" Beatrice's smile grew wider. "There are so many beautiful spots I can show you that you might not remember from when you were young."

Maddie's stomach clenched. Yes, she could turn down the offer. She could walk away. But what if that signaled to Beatrice that she did suspect her? What if this was her only chance to get a confession out of Beatrice, and find out once and for all what happened to Helen?

"That would be lovely, thanks." Maddie forced a smile as she ran her fingertips over her phone in her pocket. She navigated from memory to the redial button, relieved that the last person she had called was Jake. If she did manage to get Beatrice to confess, he would hear every word of it, likely on his voicemail.

"Wonderful. Grab another paddle if you like, I'll get the boat ready." Beatrice turned and walked over to the boat.

Maddie's heart pounded as she wondered if she should really get into the boat with her. Before she could decide, Beatrice had summoned her to step in. She found herself out in the middle of the water within moments, certain that she had made a poor decision. There was only one option. She needed to get Beatrice talking.

"Beatrice, I want to apologize again for not coming back when Chuck passed, I wish I had known." Maddie frowned.

"Please don't, darling. It's quite alright. It was a small ceremony." Beatrice shrugged. "Nothing could have made it easier, no special person, no special words. I lost my only son, my only child, and I still don't know how I'll go on without him."

"And now you've lost Helen, too." Maddie spoke carefully as she dipped the paddle into the water.

"Please don't mention her name. I don't want to speak about her." Beatrice thrust the paddle into the water harder than needed.

CHAPTER 27

A crackle of fear carried through Maddie, as sharp as Beatrice's movements as she sliced the paddle through the water.

"I'm sorry. I'd much rather talk about Chuck, if that's okay." Maddie's hand tightened around the paddle. She could feel tension coming off Beatrice in waves. Whether or not she was involved in Helen's murder, she was certainly angry.

"I keep thinking back to the times I saw him the happiest. He loved working in the shop. When his father first started letting him serve customers, he was so proud. I saw the two of them bond like I never thought possible. It was such a beautiful moment." Beatrice winced. "We planned to always keep the surf shop in the family, even if it went to a family member on my late husband's side. I only regret that Chuck never had a child to pass the shop on to. Of course that was her doing as well. She didn't want to have children." She huffed. "No one wants to have children, it's just part of life."

Maddie bit into her bottom lip and resisted the desire to correct her. She had wanted to have her children, very much. But her own experience didn't matter as much as what Beatrice had just shared with her. Even though Beatrice claimed she didn't want to talk about Helen, she obviously had so much anger toward her that she couldn't help but mention her.

"It can be so hard when your children become adults, to let them make their own choices, even when you think they might be mistakes." Maddie shook her head. "Is that how you felt about Helen?"

"Never mind her." Beatrice sighed. "She's gone now. I come out here to think about Chuck. You know Chuck was always trying to help out those who were less fortunate than him. He took Benjamin Billings right under his wing, despite his past. He didn't judge people for things like that. He told me that he was secretly supporting their bid for the amusement park." She sighed as she looked out over the wide expanse of water. "That was probably the decision that cost him his life."

"What do you mean by that?" Maddie sat forward some in the boat, careful not to rock it.

"I mean, I believe my daughter-in-law discovered that he had been supporting her opposition, and that she didn't like it. And she wanted his money, his life-

insurance. I think she found a way to get rid of him."
Beatrice's voice wavered as she spoke those words. "I
warned him time and time again that she was no good
for him. But he wouldn't listen. He never listened to
my advice when it came to her. He insisted that he was
in love." She rolled her eyes. "I don't know what he
ever saw in her."

"Chuck was always such a kind person with a good
heart." Maddie smiled. "I'm sure that he saw
something wonderful in her, something that not
everyone else could see."

"Or he imagined it." Beatrice narrowed her eyes.
"He didn't like to be wrong, either. I think he just
didn't want to admit that he'd made a mistake."

"So, you really think that she might have done
something to harm him?" Maddie's voice softened as
she realized the maddening grief she would feel, if she
was forced to see the murderer of her child each day
and pretend that everything was fine. Was that what
Beatrice had been experiencing since Chuck's death?

"No one wants me to say that." Beatrice rested the
paddle across her knees. "They all want me to pretend
that Chuck simply died of natural causes. But they
didn't see the Helen that I saw. They didn't know how
cruel she could be."

"You did," Maddie whispered. "You knew what
she was capable of, but it was impossible to prove that
she had done anything to him."

"Exactly. I tried to get people to listen to me, but it

didn't work. So, instead I just had to keep my mouth shut about it." Beatrice smirked as she looked across the boat at her. "But now, I guess I don't have to worry about that anymore." She took a deep breath and tipped her head toward the sky. "Funny how things work out sometimes."

"Very." Maddie's mouth went dry as she wondered if she should push her further. "Once, my son disappeared in a crowd of people outside of a store. I had my younger daughter in my arms and I let go of his hand for just a second." She winced. "It was the worst few moments of my life, and I was absolutely certain that someone had taken him. I was so angry, furious, and I knew that if I got my hands on the person who took him, I would tear that person to pieces!" She sighed. "Then I spotted him standing next to another mother with a baby in her arms, and I realized, no one had hurt him, no one had taken him. I was so relieved. But I never forgot how I felt during those moments. Not just the fear I felt that made me never make that mistake again, but also the fury. I knew then I was capable of far more than I ever realized."

"It's nice that your story has a good ending." Beatrice began paddling the boat back toward the edge of the water. "But mine doesn't."

"I'm just trying to say, sometimes our fear, our anger, our emotions, invent a reality that doesn't actually exist. I was so certain that he'd been taken, but he hadn't." Maddie helped steer the boat up to the dock.

"So, you're saying that I don't have a grasp on reality?" Beatrice raised an eyebrow.

"Beatrice, I'm just saying that maybe it's time you let go of that anger. You may never know the truth, and it will only hurt you to hold onto your suspicions." Maddie steadied the boat as Beatrice stepped out.

"Oh, darling." Beatrice extended her hand to her to help her out of the boat. As her long fingers tightened around Maddie's hand she smiled. "I'm not holding onto anything anymore. What's done, is finally done."

As Maddie stepped onto the dock beside her, she noted a hint of joy in Beatrice's eyes. Whether or not she had anything to do with Helen's death, it certainly had been freeing for her.

"Ladies!" Jake called out from the end of the dock. His eyes locked to Maddie's.

"Jake, what are you doing here?" Beatrice tied the boat off, then straightened up.

"Just thought I'd check in with you, Beatrice." Jake crossed his arms as he shifted his attention to her. "I know this is a difficult time for you."

"If one more person tells me how to feel, I think I'll lose my mind." Beatrice threw her hands up in the air, then laughed. "I'm just fine, Chief, thank you." She gave him a pat on his shoulder as she walked past him.

Jake tipped his hat to her, then walked toward Maddie.

She could sense his determination in his stride.

"Sorry, Jake, I thought she might say something incriminating." Maddie fished her phone out of her purse and ended the call that she now realized had never gone to voicemail. Jake had listened the entire time.

"Or you realized the danger you put yourself in getting on that boat and thought it might be a good idea to let someone know?" Jake gazed into her eyes. "What if she really had confessed to something? Do you think you both would have made it back to land?"

"It doesn't matter, she didn't confess." Maddie shrugged. "Do you think there's anything to her belief that Helen killed Chuck?"

"It's possible. But we could never prove anything." Jake glanced over his shoulder as Beatrice's car pulled out of the driveway. "Not an ounce of evidence of foul play. She knows that."

"Do you think she had something to do with Helen's murder?" Maddie frowned.

"I can't discuss that right now. I was on my way to Peter's house with a search warrant when I got your call. Please, Maddie, just go home. Stay away from Peter, take the night off, and we'll sort through things in the morning, alright?" Jake placed his hand on her shoulder and stared straight into her eyes. "Don't scare me like you did just now. If I hadn't heard the paddles in the water, I never would have known where you were."

"I'm okay, Jake." Maddie rested her hand on top of his for just a second before they both pulled away. "Are you going to arrest Peter?"

"It's just a search warrant." Jake cleared his throat. "Hopefully, he won't put up too much of a fight."

"Maybe I should go with you, I could talk to him, calm him down." Maddie stepped closer to him.

"Go home, Maddie, please." Jake turned and walked back toward his patrol car.

CHAPTER 28

*L*eft alone on the dock, Maddie stared at Helen's house. She had a feeling that Helen kept as many secrets as Craig had, but perhaps much darker ones. If there was any shred of truth to the idea that Helen had killed Chuck, she wanted to find it.

Maddie grabbed some gloves and a small flashlight from her trunk, then headed back to Helen's house just as the last of the sunlight disappeared. She found a key under the mat by the back door and let herself into the house. She didn't dare to turn any lights on in case Nancy noticed. It seemed odd to her that she didn't notice more on the day Helen had been killed. For being such a nosy neighbor, the one day when her insight would be helpful, she didn't seem to know anything. For all she knew that was because Nancy knew exactly what happened to Helen.

Maddie noticed a small office off the front hallway. She headed inside. With the flashlight clutched between her teeth, she began to sort through the papers on the desk. It was easy to recognize them as financial documents, since she had been wading through the chaos of her own financial situation ever since Craig was arrested. As she shuffled through them, she came across some information about the surf shop. In particular, the fact that Helen had intended to sell it. She'd gotten the paperwork ready and had notes about a few interested buyers.

"Oh Helen, how could you?" She frowned as she read over the notes. "Chuck would have been so upset." It dawned on her that Beatrice would have been, too. She wanted more than anything to keep the surf shop in the family. She pulled out her phone to send a message about the paperwork to Jake. Just as she unlocked it, something struck her hard on her wrist. The phone flew out of her hand.

"Leave it!" A voice commanded, inches away from her.

Beatrice?

Maddie could make out the silhouette of a baseball bat in a tall woman's hands as she lifted it over her shoulder. She quickly realized that it wasn't Beatrice.

"Shirley, no!" She jumped back as she gasped.

"I'm sorry, Maddie. You never should have come back here. I never wanted you to get mixed up in all of this. I came here to try and find proof that Helen had killed Chuck. I want to prove to everyone that she deserved to die. I want the truth to come out about what she did. But instead I found you being even more nosy." Shirley sighed as she lowered the bat some. "When Beatrice just told me about the story of your son that you told her on the boat, I decided to leave you alone, to let you live. I thought you might actually understand Beatrice's pain, her grief. And why I did what I did for her. But clearly, you didn't. You just won't leave this alone, will you?"

"Shirley, why did you kill Helen?" Maddie took a slight step back.

"She killed my nephew! She killed Chuck." Shirley scowled.

"She didn't kill Chuck!" Maddie held up her hands as the woman raised the baseball bat again. "I know you don't believe that, but it's the truth!"

"It's a lie! And I have the proof!" Shirley nodded. "I met up with Helen after Beatrice had left. I demanded to know the truth. I needed to know the truth for Beatrice, it was eating her up inside. I had to help her."

"What? What proof do you have?" Maddie stumbled over her words.

"I recorded our conversation before I killed her. She admitted to me that she slipped extra medication into his food." Shirley's voice raised even louder. "She killed him."

"What? Why didn't you show the proof to the

police? Why didn't you play them the recording?" Maddie gasped. Was Shirley lying?

"I couldn't do anything with the proof because the conversation was recorded just before I killed Helen. What I had done would have been obvious. She ruined my sister's life." Shirley shrieked her words. "Helen took the one thing that has ever made Beatrice happy from her. She took Chuck from her! She took everything from her! Helen showed up with those hideous roses for Beatrice. Helen begged her to forgive her for selling the surf shop, and to support the idea of the resort, like that even mattered!"

"Beatrice must have been devastated." Maddie's heart raced.

"She was, but none of that really mattered to Beatrice. All that mattered was that Chuck was dead! When Beatrice told me she had met with Helen at the dock and how upset she was, I came here to talk to Helen to stop her from ruining things even more. She was down by the dock taking photos of it. When I asked her what she was doing, she said she was taking photos of it because she was going to sell the house. I knew that would devastate Beatrice even more. I needed to help my sister get her revenge."

"So you killed Helen?" Maddie whispered.

"Beatrice thought fate would make Helen pay for what she did." Shirley shook her head. "But I knew that we had to take action. I had to take action. I needed to do what my sister wasn't strong enough to do. She was ruining my sister's life. I told her that she better sign everything over to Beatrice or I would ruin her. She laughed at me and said what did I think I could do. Something switched in her and she started bragging about killing Chuck. She said I might as well know the truth as I would never be able to prove it. Can you believe that? She admitted that she had killed Chuck. She told me that he deserved it. He was siding with Bob and Benjamin Billings behind her back. He was planning on leaving her, finally. My sister could finally have some peace, she could have her son back. He was finally going to leave her and what did Helen do, she killed him."

"That must have been terrible. You just wanted your sister to be happy." Maddie tried to appear as if she was sympathizing with her. Maybe it would buy her some time.

"It was. That's all I wanted. I knew if I killed Helen, my sister would get the surf shop, and the house, and the dock that Chuck built. She could at least have everything that was her son's, and at least still have his memories. And Helen would finally pay for what she did to Chuck. For what she did to my sister. I had to get rid of her. I grabbed the camera strap around her neck and I strangled her. I didn't know if it would work, but it did. When she collapsed and hit her head on a rock, I knew that was it. She was dead." Shirley sobbed, but the bat didn't waver in her grasp. "I did what I had to do, Maddie!"

"You don't have to do this!" Maddie's heart raced as she realized that Shirley had every intention to kill her. "I know you're not really a killer, Shirley!"

"I am!" Shirley hissed the words. "My nephew was taken away from me! My sister will never be the same! I made sure Helen got what she deserved! I'm sorry, Maddie, really I am!"

"Drop it!" Jake's voice bellowed through the small office.

Maddie dodged the swing of the bat. It missed her and slammed against the desk instead.

"Shirley!" Jake shouted again. "Drop it, or I'll shoot!"

"It doesn't matter." The bat clattered to the floor. "It doesn't matter. All that matters is that my sister got justice for Chuck. My sister got her revenge." Shirley held up her hands.

Maddie gasped as she watched Jake handcuff Shirley and lead her from the office. She couldn't believe that both Helen and Shirley were actually murderers.

After filling out paperwork and going through a medical assessment, Jake drove Maddie home. Her hands still trembled as she sat in silence beside him.

"She'll get the help she needs." Jake glanced over at her.

"Good." Maddie closed her eyes and prepared herself for a lecture.

Instead, Jake gave her shoulder a light rub. Then he turned into her driveway.

"And we have proof that Chuck was murdered. Helen certainly covered that up well." He parked in her driveway and got out of the car. "Shirley gave me a recording of the confession. Beatrice really had no idea what Shirley had done."

"I really thought Beatrice was the murderer." Maddie walked up the driveway.

Maddie smiled as Bella and Polly greeted her with their wagging tails.

"I'll get you some tea before I go." Jake didn't ask, just made himself comfortable in her kitchen.

Maddie didn't protest. Tea seemed like exactly what she needed.

As Maddie sat in one of the rocking chairs on the porch with Bella and Polly in her lap, she wondered just how he had known to be there at the right time to save her.

"Here you go." Jake handed her a cup of tea, then sat down beside her in the other rocking chair. As he looked out over the water, the tension in his face eased. "So, what do you think, are you going to stay?"

"Bayview is my home." Maddie looked over at him as the light breeze from the water tugged at the hair that feathered across his forehead. "I guess it always has been, and it looks like it always will be."

"Well." Jake sat forward in the rocking chair and

met her eyes. "We're all glad to have you. You were a hero today, Maddie."

"Me?" Maddie laughed as she shook her head. "I'm not the hero in this situation, Jake. You are. If you hadn't shown up when you did, I never would have made it out of there alive."

"The only reason I showed up when I did, is because I found out that Beatrice had been to see Benjamin Billings after Chuck's death because she had found out Helen had promised to sell the surf shop to Benjamin before Chuck's death. Helen had assured him that he would soon be the owner of it. Beatrice went to see him to say that would never happen."

"How did you find out?" Maddie rubbed her wrist. Now that the adrenalin was starting to wear off, her wrist was starting to ache from when Shirley had knocked the phone out of her hand.

"After I served the search warrant on Peter's house, I went straight to Benjamin to find out just how close he and Chuck were. He admitted to Helen's offer, and his own suspicions that she had something to do with Chuck's murder. Beatrice had found out about the offer and she said that was proof that Helen had planned to get rid of Chuck. She had been telling him ever since Chuck's death that Helen had killed Chuck, and that she would pay for what she did. He had hoped that it was just talk. But he played an irate voicemail for me, that Beatrice left, when she found out that Helen intended to sell the surf shop."

"So, you knew something was wrong?" Maddie ran her hands through the dogs' fur.

"Yes, I thought it was Beatrice, though. I had no idea that Shirley was the murderer. But that was why I ended up at Helen's house, to see if I could find the paperwork that you had already discovered. We hadn't taken it in as evidence when we searched the place, because we didn't think it was relevant to Helen's murder. I'm just glad I wasn't too late." Jake frowned.

"Poor Beatrice. Now, she's lost her sister as well." Maddie shook her head.

"I doubt that Shirley thought about that when she murdered Helen. I'm sure she thought that she was helping her sister. Getting justice for Chuck." Jake stood up from the rocking chair, then held his hand out to her. "Good work, Maddie."

Maddie smiled as she took his hand in a firm shake. "I thought you might be angry with me." She held his hand longer than necessary, though he showed no sign of pulling it away.

"Oh, I can tell you that if you ever put yourself in a position to be harmed again, I'm going to be plenty angry." Jake tensed his jaw. "But I can't be angry at you for trying to find out the truth. For being one of the bravest people I know. I've always admired that about you, Maddie."

"Thank you, Jake." Maddie let her hand settle in

her lap as he turned to walk away, chased by two friendly dogs, eager to make him stay.

Jake laughed as he knelt down to give each one a pet. The warmth in his eyes obvious. After one more glance over his shoulder, he walked off to his car.

As Maddie watched him back out of the driveway, her phone beeped with a text. She looked down at it to see it was from her son, Dean.

Mom. Is it okay if I come visit you before I start the new job?

Maddie felt a rush of excitement at the thought of seeing him. She missed the time they spent together. Why was he coming to visit her all of a sudden? He probably wanted to check on her. She smiled as she sent him a text.

Of course. I can't wait to see you.

She summoned Bella and Polly to her side, then looked out over the bay. Maybe things had changed quite a bit in Bayview, but now that the murder had been solved, she was excited to invite children and grandchildren to visit. She hadn't expected that her sister and son would be visiting so soon and she couldn't wait to see them.

For the first time in a long time, Maddie was looking forward to what the future would bring.

The End

MADDIE'S CHOCOLATE CUPCAKE RECIPE

Ingredients:

Cupcakes:

1 cup all-purpose flour
3/4 teaspoon baking powder
1/2 teaspoon baking soda
1/4 teaspoon salt
1/2 cup unsweetened cocoa powder
1/2 cup granulated sugar
1/2 cup light brown sugar
2 large eggs, at room temperature
1/4 cup vegetable or canola oil
1 teaspoon vanilla extract
3/4 cup buttermilk, at room temperature

Chocolate Buttercream Frosting:

2 sticks (1 cup) unsalted butter, softened to room temperature
3 to 3 1/2 cups confectioners' sugar
3 to 4 tablespoons milk
1/2 cup unsweetened cocoa powder
1 teaspoon vanilla extract
1/4 teaspoon salt

Preparation:

Preheat the oven to 350 degrees Fahrenheit.

Line the muffin pans with paper cupcake liners. This recipe makes 14 cupcakes.

Sift the flour, baking powder, baking soda, salt and cocoa powder into a bowl. Add the sugars and stir to combine.

In another bowl beat together the eggs, oil, vanilla extract and buttermilk until combined.
Gradually add the wet ingredients to the dry ingredients. Mix until combined.

Divide between the cupcake liners.

Bake for 15 to 18 minutes or until a skewer inserted into the middle comes out clean.

Leave to cool in the pan for 10 minutes, then transfer to a wire rack to cool completely.

To prepare the chocolate buttercream frosting, beat the butter for about two to three minutes, until creamy.

Add 3 cups of the confectioners' sugar, 3 tablespoons of the milk, cocoa powder, vanilla extract and salt. Beat until well-combined and fluffy. To get the desired consistency, gradually add more milk, if too thick, or add more confectioners' sugar, if too thin.

Spoon or pipe the frosting on top of the cupcakes.

Enjoy!!

ABOUT THE AUTHOR

Cindy Bell is a USA Today and Wall Street Journal Bestselling Author. She is the author of the Little Leaf Creek, Dune House, Chocolate Centered, Sage Gardens, Maddie Mills, Wagging Tail, Donut Truck, Macaron Patisserie, Nuts about Nuts, Bekki the Beautician, Heavenly Highland Inn and Wendy the Wedding Planner cozy mystery series.

Cindy has always loved reading, but it is only recently that she has discovered her passion for writing romantic cozy mysteries. She loves walking along the beach with her Cocker Spaniel thinking of the next adventure her characters can embark on.

You can sign up for her newsletter so you are notified of her latest releases at http://www.cindybellbooks.com.

ALSO BY CINDY BELL

MADDIE MILLS COZY MYSTERY SERIES

Slain at the Sea

Homicide at the Harbor

LITTLE LEAF CREEK COZY MYSTERY SERIES

Little Leaf Creek Cozy Mystery Series Box Set Vol 1
(Books 1 - 3)

Little Leaf Creek Cozy Mystery Series Box Set Vol 2
(Books 3 - 6)

Little Leaf Creek Cozy Mystery Series Box Set Vol 3
(Books 7 -9)

Chaos in Little Leaf Creek

Peril in Little Leaf Creek

Conflict in Little Leaf Creek

Action in Little Leaf Creek

Vengeance in Little Leaf Creek

Greed in Little Leaf Creek

Surprises in Little Leaf Creek

Missing in Little Leaf Creek

Haunted in Little Leaf Creek

CHOCOLATE CENTERED COZY MYSTERIES

WAGGING TAIL COZY MYSTERIES

SAGE GARDENS COZY MYSTERIES

NUTS ABOUT NUTS COZY MYSTERIES

DONUT TRUCK COZY MYSTERIES

Bunny Donuts and a Body

Strawberry Donuts and Scandal

Frosted Donuts and Fatal Falls

BEKKI THE BEAUTICIAN COZY MYSTERIES

Hairspray and Homicide

A Dyed Blonde and a Dead Body

Mascara and Murder

Pageant and Poison

Conditioner and a Corpse

Mistletoe, Makeup and Murder

Hairpin, Hair Dryer and Homicide

Blush, a Bride and a Body

Shampoo and a Stiff

Cosmetics, a Cruise and a Killer

Lipstick, a Long Iron and Lifeless

Camping, Concealer and Criminals

Treated and Dyed

A Wrinkle-Free Murder

A MACARON PATISSERIE COZY MYSTERY SERIES

Sifting for Suspects

Recipes and Revenge

Mansions, Macarons and Murder

HEAVENLY HIGHLAND INN COZY MYSTERIES

Murdering the Roses

Dead in the Daisies

Killing the Carnations

Drowning the Daffodils

Suffocating the Sunflowers

Books, Bullets and Blooms

A Deadly Serious Gardening Contest

A Bridal Bouquet and a Body

Digging for Dirt

WENDY THE WEDDING PLANNER COZY MYSTERIES

Matrimony, Money and Murder

Chefs, Ceremonies and Crimes

Knives and Nuptials

Mice, Marriage and Murder

Printed in Great Britain
by Amazon

86596692R00122